Absolution

Patrick T. Groome

Copyright © 2022 Patrick T. Groome

All rights reserved.

ISBN: 979 880741 147 1

For Tom and Anna.

1

Father Wyatt genuflected, crossed himself and walked briskly to the confessional. Saturday 10 a.m. He believed in God and punctuality. It was not going to be a busy morning, he could tell. There was no one waiting. There rarely was. Confession, he thought, was becoming an irrelevancy. He'd even stopped going to his own confessor some years ago, realising that he didn't feel the need of an intermediary between himself and the Almighty. God knew; Wyatt knew; nobody else needed to. But there were still those who felt the need. So he felt obliged every Saturday at 10 a.m. to make himself available.

He sometimes wondered if it made any difference: the same people with the same sins were given the same penance. For the most part the sins were small misdemeanours of little moral value: a lack of respect, a family squabble, an outburst of anger, a salacious thought. For most, the penance – a few Our Fathers or Hail Marys – was punishment enough; the conscience was salved temporarily but didn't cure the problem. Perhaps a moment's comfort was the purpose. It wouldn't really matter how many times offences were repeated, as long as there was that momentary ecstasy of the burden lifted. At times, he sat and listened at length as a parishioner used him as a bucket to pour in the slop of a life, at the end of which there was nothing to say except: "Go in peace". So he continued to make himself available every Saturday at 10a.m.

ABSOLUTION

He was idly watching a spider closing in on a fly when the door creaked and a young, female voice uttered, in a tone somewhere between a sob and a suppressed scream:

"Help me, Father. I've killed someone!"

No sooner uttered than the figure got up and left. Wyatt was taken aback, too slow to flip the curtain, too slow to leave the cramped box.

He fumbled the catch and spilled out into the aisle. He looked to his right and, just before the great west door banged to, he caught the glimpse of a lower leg wearing a red boot.

2

In a lay-by beside an old trunk road in the high Cotswolds a single-decker bus waited. It had been waiting a long time. It was a transport café. The Union flag hung limp and tattered above the driver's door. The side windows had been converted into a counter. Behind the counter a small bald-headed man, in his forties, with both forearms smudged with tattoos was gently flipping bacon on the griddle and stirring onions. It was eight o'clock Tuesday morning, mid-January. Steam rose from the bus and gently dispersed over the drystone walls and sheep as still as statues in the frosty pastures.

There was no business yet. That would come. Some regular HGVs; some regular salesmen; occasional passersby; sometimes the curious would keep him busy enough. A black Audi Quattro A3, a few years old pulled in along from the bus. The bald man glanced. Good timing, he thought. The bacon's almost done.

A well-suited man with slicked back, greying hair, approached the counter.

"Morning, my friend," chirruped the bald bacon flipper. "Will it be the full English or just a cuppa and a butty?"

"Graham. Geordie Graham?"

"Yeah, that's me. Who's asking?"

"Bellum. Parabellum," came the reply, and in a

movement quicker than the flash of a stripper's crotch, Slickedback pulled out his pistol and fired.

The bullet entered Geordie Graham's right eye. Blood splattered. A window shattered. The bacon sizzled gently on the griddle.

3

Detective Inspector Kate Brown was running late for work. Her seven year old daughter, Misha, had looked a little pale, was complaining of a cold and seemed too ill to go to school, so Kate decided to see if her mum would be able to drop over for the day. That would be three days in a row. Granny often helped when Kate had weekend shifts. Granny was delighted, as always, to help. She knew what it was like to be a single parent herself, and would have loved to have spent even more time with Misha and Kate, if Kate had allowed it. But Kate knew her own limits and tolerances, both physical and personal. So Granny had learnt to manage her disappointment and enjoy the moments that they did share.

"I'll be back about six," said Kate, biting into buttered toast, grabbing a bag, phone, keys and opening a door in one movement. "Bye, Misha. Get well soon. Thanks, Mum," and with that the door slammed.

Granny and Misha looked at each other and smiled like conspirators.

4

The morning briefing was just breaking up, so Kate went straight to her office and fired up the computer. A knock at the door.

"Ma'am."

"Yes, Sergeant."

Sergeant Joe Sheldon was twenty eight, smart in appearance, smart in intellect. Red brick university and fast-tracked. His mum thought him cuddly, his girlfriend thought him handsome and his immediate boss, Kate, thought he was as tough as nuts under the smooth exterior. She liked him.

"Not a great deal new, ma'am," started Joe. "A couple of break-ins on South Side Industrial Estate. B Team is looking into them. Report of a conman on Summer Heights. Usual thing. Water, gas, electricity check at an elderly person's home. That's come to me. Oh, and the mayor's wife called again demanding why we haven't taken any action over her cat. She was not impressed with our triage system. Stolen cats, according to her, should have priority over stolen cars. And when Sergeant Benson suggested the cat might have had a good reason to leave home, she went ballistic, threatened to have Benson disciplined and said that the superintendent would soon be hearing from the mayor."

Kate smiled and shook her head. She could imagine

the discussion between Superintendent Fordyce and Councillor Johnny Thompson, two old school friends, golf club members as well as numerous other social and political connections. There would be chumminess and politeness, out of which would come a clear commitment to dedicate the force's reserves to the solving of that deepest, most intriguing, indeed most heinous crime: the Case of the Wandering Pussy.

"Thanks, Joe. I'll update this report on the night club stabbing, get to the hospital and catch up with you later.

"Yes, ma'am." Joe turned and left.

Kate's phone rang.

"Inspector Brown. Superintendent Fordyce here. I have a job for you."

5

Without hesitating, Father Wyatt ran to the door and, reaching the street, glanced left to see a red-booted woman walking briskly away about a hundred metres ahead. From that distance he could make out that she was of medium height and wore a black ribbed down jacket. There was a suggestion of blonde hair under a black woollen pom-pom. He didn't dare estimate an age. He had only the memory of her voice to go on.

She turned into a high street supermarket.

It was then that Father Wyatt hesitated. What was he trying to do? A woman, young, he thought, had just confessed to a murder. That certainly was unusual. He'd not had that one before. He had had plenty of strange ones including attempted bestiality and guilt over various fetishes but why did he get up and begin to follow this one? He had nothing to go on. He didn't recognise the voice. As far as he knew she had not been to St. Jude's before. No details. Nothing. Was she even telling the truth? Was she unhinged? He could tell from her voice that she was distressed, but she wouldn't have been the first deranged person to drop in on a Saturday and he had never before felt the actual urge to follow someone.

In any case, he pretty well knew the kinds of people he dealt with as a shop assistant knows the buying habits of customers. And though still in his thirties and still young for a priest, he thought himself pretty unshockable in the same way as a teacher, police officer or social worker can become inured to the desperate end of human nature and are not shocked by the capacity of people to do or to suffer extraordinary things.

He was genuinely surprised at himself. There was something urgent, engaging and – dare he admit it? – attractive about the way she had confessed that stirred in him a call to action, a desire to help, a need to save, a deep curiosity to know more. He still didn't quite understand what he was doing as he walked down the street to the supermarket.

He tried to look casual as he picked up a wire basket but he knew he must have looked like a meerkat on sentry duty as he scanned the rows and aisles trying to catch a glimpse of her.

He dropped a couple of loose apples and a bunch of bananas into his basket and headed along to the cheese and cooked meats. By the milk trolleys at the end he stopped. There she was! Two aisles along by the domestic cleaning products. She was scanning the shelves hurriedly, selecting items, seemingly at random, but Wyatt could see that in her basket, bleach, gloves, scourers and other things suggested a clear theme: this woman has some serious cleaning to do.

In an attempt to get a clearer look at her face, Wyatt approached the aisle. His intention was to walk by, take a quick glance, then consider his next move. However, at the same time he glanced, she turned and met him full gaze. Her bright blue eyes widened and her mouth made a small o in surprise. In Wyatt something stirred, first in his heart, then in his loins.

ABSOLUTION

"Let me help," were the first words he uttered.

6

Summer Heights used to be a council estate which had begun life in the late nineteen-forties on green belt land to the side of a small market town. It had grown fast to house families displaced by the Second World War. Now some of the houses were privately owned, some were privately tenanted and the rest belonged to either housing associations or the council. Despite the worthy cultural intentions of the good burghers to name the streets after long-forgotten poets and essayists, there was little elevation of the spirits the further you went into the estate.

It began with colourful promise in Steele Drive; you could sense the pride in Dryden Avenue; Pope Gardens offered hope but who knows what Joseph Addison would have thought of the street that bore his name: small terraces or semi-detached houses; picket fences with broken palings; ragged privet hedges; metal-framed windows with broken panes; wheelie bins strewn on front gardens and the number of the house daubed in white paint to the side of the door.

It was at the door of number 35 that Sergeant Joe Sheldon was standing. He knocked again.

A tetchy voice replied, "Hang on, will yer. I'm getting there."

Sheldon heard the rattle of a chain and the clunk of a sliding bolt.

A man in a wheelchair appeared. He was bulky and had thinning grey hair. In his sixties, Sheldon guessed.

"Yeah. What do you want?"

"Good morning, Mr. Wentworth. I'm Detective Sergeant Sheldon," said Sheldon holding out his ID, giving Wentworth enough time to scrutinise it. "I'm following up on the incident regarding an unwelcome visitor."

"Oh, right. You'd better come in".

Wentworth deftly turned his wheelchair and led the way along a small hallway, past the stairlift, to a sitting room on the left.

Sheldon's first impression was of gentle neglect, not so much grubbiness as tiredness: dingy wallpaper, worn settee, the stale smell of fried food but, surprisingly to Sheldon, no dust. There was some pride left, Sheldon thought.

Wentworth pointed to the settee. Sheldon sat down and began:

"Do you live alone, Mr. Wentworth?"

"What's that got to do with it?" retorted Wentworth.

"I couldn't help noticing. It's nice and tidy. No dust. I just wondered if anyone else lives here."

"No, nobody. I have a cleaner. I do what I can myself."

"Right. Thank you. Would you tell me what

happened?", said Sheldon, taking out his notebook and clicking his pen.

"Yeah, well. Friday. It was Friday I phoned in and you've just come now. The bugger'll be long gone, or done someone else."

"If you would just tell me what happened," replied Sheldon politely yet firmly.

Wentworth shook his head. His jowls wobbled like tripe on a butcher's tray.

"Well, I get a knock on the door. This bloke with a blue overall flashed a card at me and said he had to check the utilities. Well I was having a problem with the boiler and I was expecting someone from the housing association to come round. So I let him in. I went to the kitchen to make a cup of tea. He said he had to check meters, boiler, sockets and taps, so I said to him to go round and do what he had to do."

Sheldon wrote quickly, nodding at Wentworth, "And how long was he here?"

"After about fifteen minutes he said he was done, had everything, said I'd be hearing from the association shortly, that I needn't worry and he would show himself out."

"Did he go upstairs as well?"

"Yeah, everywhere."

"And then what happened?"

"It was only after he left that I thought it was a bit funny, so I started checking around. I haven't got anything really valuable and I keep no cash in the house, but I thought I'd look anyway. Everything seemed to be in order upstairs. And the same downstairs till I came in here and noticed that the frame had gone."

"Anything special about the frame?" asked Sheldon.

"As it happens that was the most valuable thing in the house. It's a Victorian, solid silver picture frame. Used to belong to my mum and her mum before that. Gone. Priceless." Anger mounted in Wentworth's voice. "What's more it's got the only picture of my son. If I get my hands on that bastard there's no saying what I'll do to him."

"Is the frame insured, Mr. Wentworth?"

"What's that got to do with it?" replied Wentworth, spittle appearing on his lower lip.

"Well, if it is, there's likely to be a full description, and possibly a photo of it. That can help with tracing and identifying it."

Wentworth wheeled himself over to a bureau and rummaged. In a moment he handed over an envelope which contained insurance details, a photo of the frame and a valuation given ten years before.

"Thanks, Mr. Wentworth. If I may, I'll take this, make a copy and return it in a day or two. Now perhaps you could describe the visitor."

Wentworth blew out his lips. "Well I didn't really take

any notice. He had a blue overall and wore a woolly hat. He was about medium height, not thin not fat. Didn't see his hair. He looked as though he needed a shave. Can't think of anything else."

"Did he have an accent? What did he sound like? Did he use any particular words, or say anything in an unusual way?"

"No, I don't think so. Just ordinary like."

"Well, Mr. Wentworth. Thank you for being so helpful. If you think of anything else you can reach me on this number," said Sheldon handing him a card. "I'll be back in a day or two to return the insurance details. Don't trouble yourself. I'll see myself out."

As he closed the front door behind him, Sheldon thought: There is something odd about that house. But he couldn't put his finger on what it was.

7

Chartlebury Station looked glorious in the pale sunlight. The winter sun brought warmth to the pale limestone of the entrance hall and ticket office. The yellows, reds, purples and greens of the winter pansies in baskets and beds festooned the two platforms. Pride exuded; pleasure felt. The name of the station on each of the platforms stood out in white relief against a warm mid-brown background. The overall impression was of charm and solidity, dependability and certainty.

Cindy Graham, age forty five, stood wrapped against the winter chill. A scarf covered her mouth, and though the pale sun did not warrant it, she wore dark sunglasses. She had a small suitcase in one hand and in the other a one-way ticket. She had good reason to leave. She was not coming back.

8

The first thing she saw was his dog collar.

"Father," she stammered, a look of panic crossing her face. "I ...er..." She made to move.

"Stay, please," said Wyatt, taking hold of her basket. "Let's take these and go somewhere to talk."

Wyatt paid for the fruit and cleaning stuff.

Five minutes later, in the corner of Mama's Italian Café, the two sat opposite each other. She had a latte in front of her, Wyatt an americano.

"I can help," said Wyatt. "Tell me your name. Just start at the beginning." His voice was gentle, confident and sincere.

"Alice. Sometimes Ali but Father..."

"Call me, Tom."

"Tom," she ventured uncertainly. She took a deep breath then out tumbled word over word, "I panicked. I didn't know what to do. I knew it was wrong. I shouldn't have done it. He's dead. I did it. I shouldn't have. He's dead. He's dead...he's dead."

Wyatt looked at the moist blue eyes framed by the oval of her face and the natural blonde hair. He took in her soft complexion, lightly freckled nose, full lips and white teeth.

"Alice, when did this happen?" Wyatt's calmness was beginning to have an effect.

Alice took a deep breath. "This morning, early on. I must go." She got up to leave.

"Stay, Alice," Wyatt's hand gently but firmly touched her forearm. "Just a little longer." She sat down, exhausted. "I'll help. It was probably an accident."

"No, I meant to do it. I wanted him dead. He's cheated on me once too often."

And then it all poured out. How they'd met a couple of years ago, had fun, decided to live together. Then the drinking, the late nights, the secretive phone calls, the missing money, the challenges, the unexplained absences, the forgiveness, the starting over, the repeating cycle.

"Finally, last night, that was it. The last straw. He came in about three o'clock, drunk, strong with another woman's perfume. I just lost it. He turned away. I picked up with both hands the cast iron frying pan and smashed his skull. I left him there, lifeless on the kitchen floor."

"You came to confession about ten," said Wyatt."So what did you do in the meantime?"

"I just wandered around. It was cold but I was wrapped up. I went to the market café early morning. It was busy from about five. I didn't know what to do. I was going mad with worry and guilt. I needed to tell someone, but who could I tell? I went to confession. I thought it would help. I was confused. I felt guilty and innocent at the same time. I can't explain it. As soon as I went in I realised that was useless. What I needed to do was be practical, to clean up, to make it look like an accident, maybe move the body, to pretend it didn't happen. I don't know."

And from the depths of her fatigue broke forth the long sobs of guilt, remorse, relief, acceptance and futility. Her shoulders heaved and she wailed.

9

Kate took out her notebook and flicked through it. On her computer she scanned the witness reports which had been input by the two interviewing officers. Her job entailed pulling together all the information into a cogent report, summarising and clarifying where necessary and planning next steps. On the face of it, it was a straightforward enough crime: an assault with lots of witnesses.

The previous Friday night about 10 p.m. there was a disturbance outside The Black Cat night club. There were a lot of young people, mainly mid-twenties, drunk, high and with plenty of cash out for the usual Friday night hi-jinks. The Black Cat was popular. It was a well-run establishment with strict drug and behaviour policies. Its reputation was of high-spiritedness rather than rowdiness.

The witness statements confirmed that there was the usual good banter in the queue waiting to get in. Then, suddenly, quite unexpectedly, there was a push and a shove, the doorman fell to the floor, blood oozing through his white dress shirt. The screams and commotion brought the manager and a couple of members of staff who managed the situation as well as they could until the ambulance and the police arrived.

Kate arrived at the same time as the ambulance and another patrol car. The doorman had been stabbed, was unable to talk and was taken straight to the hospital where he remained under sedation in the intensive care unit.

Kate read through the statements again. There was a lot about the atmosphere before and after the incident, but not one was clear about exactly what happened. No one had actually seen the stabbing. No one could say who was at the front of the queue; everybody was behind somebody else. No one had any mobile footage. In the manager's office later, Kate had looked at the CCTV images but there was little to go on there. Black and white grainy images revealed no more than the witness statements.

Kate spoke further with the manager, a Mr. Paul Levinson, who gave the details of the assaulted doorman.

Ritchie Goodwin had been working Fridays and Saturdays for the past six months He was young, 25, fit and tall. He was of mixed West Indian and white heritage. He got on well with the customers; he could banter but would know when to be serious. No one dared to challenge him. He knew where and how to draw the line and the club goers knew well where that line was. He had been recommended by George Stevens, the owner of the club.

Kate finished her summary. A serious assault but nothing to go on. It was time to see if Ritchie Goodwin was fit to help.

10

Mrs. Elaine Thompson sat in her lounge with a cup of coffee in her hand. She was looking out of the French windows over her garden, across the school fields to the distant hills beyond. She liked her house, a detached mid-seventies, light brick, executive dwelling on an estate of small closes. Her house was at the end of Laurel Close and adjoined the secondary school playing fields. Because of the siting of trees and shrubs she could not see the school buildings in the distance. She barely heard the pupils even in the summer time. Only rarely did a pupil approach her laurel hedge boundary for, if she did see anyone, she was quick to act.

Soon after she moved in she made it perfectly clear to the head teacher that that part of the school fields was out of bounds. After several long, persistent telephone calls in which Mrs. Thompson asserted her rights to respect, privacy and tranquillity and in which she emphasised stridently that she was the wife of Johnny Thompson, prominent local councillor, the head teacher capitulated and the area beyond her back hedge was deemed out of bounds.

The view comforted her. It made her feel that she owned and controlled all that she saw. She imagined herself living in the countryside with all the advantages that a town could bring. For someone who had been brought up on Summer Heights this, she thought, was about as good as it got.

However comforting the view, it could not soothe that morning her inner anxiety. She was very worried about her cat. It was not like Marmalade, usually known as Marmy, not to return. She had mentioned it to her neighbour, who had talked about a gang of catnappers reputedly prowling the area stealing cats to order. Mrs. Thompson had got it into her head that that must indeed be the case so had postered local lamp posts and had contacted the school. She had also phoned the police. No one seemed to care. No Marmy appeared.

If she had looked more deeply into her anxiety she might have found that she was also worried about her husband and her son.

She was proud of her husband, an estate agent with several offices in town and the neighbouring larger villages. She also loved her son. No mother could love a son more. Her reflections were broken by the sound of the front door opening.

"Lee, darling, is that you?" She heard footsteps on the parquet hall floor heading to the kitchen. "Lee. Lee. Are you there?" her voice rising. She got up and went to the kitchen door and stopped. "Oh, Lee. It is you. Why didn't you answer darling? I didn't know who it might be at this time. I wasn't expecting you. It's only eleven. I didn't hear you come in last night. Are you alright darling?"

A tall person with medium length brown hair and wearing a black leather bomber jacket with a white silk scarf slammed the door of the American-style refrigerator and turned to face his mother.

"Oh do shut up mother. Why is there never enough milk in this house?" He made to move past her. "Get out of the way. I've got things to do."

"But darling you look so pale. Are you ill? Is there anything I can do?"

"Yes," he said, lowering his head until their noses nearly touched, looking hard into her eyes. "Get out of my way. Then get out of my life."

Elaine stepped back stunned. Her eyes filled, her lower lips quivered, her stomach knotted and she began to wet herself.

11

As the town grew so did the hospital. What started life as a compact building set in extensive, ornamental grounds on the principle that the body better heals when the spirit is uplifted, was now a labyrinth. The ornamental gardens had long given way to car parks and extensions. The building was a sprawling mass of arms and legs of corridors. If there had been logic in its first design, it was difficult to decipher it now, Kate thought, as she entered the lobby. The wall of signs, colours and arrows that met her would have been overwhelming to someone coming in for the first time, but Kate had been here many times before. She turned left for the general reception.

Kate held out her ID but the woman at the desk knew her, smiled, waved and nodded. Left again then right down a long corridor with bays, some with chairs, some with beds, past doors with 'No Entry. Hazard.' The corridors were busy with medics, patients and visitors; with gurneys and trolleys and quick-stepping nurses. Finally, Kate turned to the right and twenty metres later reached the intensive care reception.

It was like leaving a busy motorway and turning into a quiet cul-de-sac. The overall impression was of calmness and purpose. A young nurse sat at the desk, jotting something down on an official looking form.

Kate presented her ID. "I'm here for an update on Ritchie Goodwin. I'd like to speak with him if I can."

"I'm sorry," the nurse replied. "That won't be possible. Mr. Goodwin died twenty minutes ago."

That makes it murder, thought Kate, and if it had been possible her determination factor notched one level higher. "Have the next of kin been informed?"

"Dr. Singh is talking to his mother now. I'll tell them you're here."

Fifteen minutes later, Kate was in a small side room, a cross between a waiting room and a cleaner's cupboard. On the wall was a black and white blow up photograph of the hospital as it looked in the nineteen thirties. On the steps stood the staff primly exuding earnestness. A doctor, one supposed, thumbs in waistcoat, was flanked by two nurses with large white hats and long uniform dresses and to the side, slightly apart was a patient in a wheelchair. In the corner of the room was a beaten, chipped and scuffed Henry vacuum cleaner on whose face hardly a smile remained and whose eyes were dimmed with the grime of ages. There were two plastic chairs on which sat Kate and Mrs. Goodwin, facing each other, their knees nearly touching.

"I am so sorry, Mrs. Goodwin," began Kate. "I won't keep you long, but if you can tell me what you can about what might have led to this, that will help."

Mrs. Goodwin, pale, drawn and exhausted looked towards Kate. "I don't understand it," she muttered. "I don't understand it at all. He was such a good boy. Who would do that to him?"

Gently, Kate responded, "Do you know anyone that might have wished him harm?"

"He was such a good boy. Never in trouble. Well-liked. He worked hard at school. He was good at sports." Mrs. Goodwin's head moved softly from side to side as though she was trying to think and make sense of it all. "He didn't go out a lot, except to the gym. He had girls as friends but no special one. He had two jobs, you know. He wanted his own business one day. Something to do with sports – maybe a shop, maybe a fitness centre".

Kate added, "He recently started work at the night club. Was that one of the two jobs? They spoke well of him there. Where was his main job?"

"He works for Kenwick Enterprises, for a Mr. George Stevens. Ritchie's the office manager," she emphasised the *the*. "Well, was," her voice lowering.

"How long had he'd been working there?" encouraged Kate.

"Since leaving school. He could have gone to university. He had the grades, but Ritchie wanted to get out in the real world, to earn money, to learn business. He was always good with figures."

"So he's an accountant."

"Well everything really. He started off at Town and Country Motors then went on to Thompson and Thompson Estate Agents, then on to Industrial

Warehousing Limited and then Kenwick Enterprises."

"Why all the changes?" queried Kate.

"Well, they're not really changes. All the businesses are owned by Mr. Stevens. A lovely man. He took a real shine to Ritchie from the time Ritchie asked him, as a kid, if he could wash his car for him for a charity fundraiser. He did such a good job, he was invited to wash his car regularly until he got too old to do it. Treated him like a son. Ritchie lost his dad to cancer when he was thirteen. Mr. Stevens said he would show him how to run a business and then one day he would know enough to set up on his own." Mrs. Goodwin took a deep breath, like a swimmer might, coming up for air.

"Thank you, Mrs. Goodwin. I won't keep you long. Just one more thing."

"Do you know of anyone who might have wanted to harm Ritchie?"

For answer, Mrs. Goodwin began to shake her head. Her shoulders heaved and from the depth of her being there came a long, sonorous, single note. Then came the tears.

Kate left her seat and put her arms around Mrs. Goodwin's shoulders.

.

12

As the train trundled past the low, wet fields on the way to Paddington, Cindy Graham began to relax. And with the relaxation came the reflection on the hand that fate had dealt her.

At sixteen, her aspirations were to leave the cramped terrace in Aldershot and to get married. In Aldershot, the quickest way to escape was to marry a squaddie and get a subsidised house. There were a lot of girls who thought like that. At the weekends the discos and pubs were always packed; the soldiers had money to burn and things to prove. There was a lot of fun and if a grope in an alleyway or a car at the end of evening was the price of escape, then so be it. One night she thought she had met the right guy. She was eighteen. That guy was Geordie Graham, private soldier, Royal Logistic Corps.

Geordie, too, had wanted to escape. He adored his mum, quite liked his step-dad but he wanted to become a driver and to see the world. At sixteen he joined up; at seventeen he was on driving courses; at eighteen he had his parts 1 and 2; and at 21 he could drive anything the army gave him.

The green airfields of England, the country byways, busy motorways and the tracks on Salisbury Plain soon gave way to the mountains of Bosnia then, later the sands of Iraq and Afghanistan. The open road then didn't seem so appealing.

On leave when he was nineteen he married Cindy, a rumbustious affair. When the haze had worn off they squeezed into their married quarters – a terraced house with damp, crumbling plaster and leaky taps. New houses were on the way, they were told; but for Cindy it felt like she had never escaped.

They had two children in quick succession. The pressure of space, the disappointment of hopes unfulfilled, the growing moodiness of Geordie began to tell. Verbal arguments led to physical blows. Cindy looked forward to the times he was posted abroad, four or six month tours, but dreaded the returns. She thought of leaving, but with two children where would she go? She confided in her friends, other soldiers' wives, and realised she was not alone.

Geordie, too, was not happy. He never spoke about his war experiences, but Cindy noticed his mood swings becoming more severe: high elation, deep depression; a lot of drink, a lot of anger; some tears and some regret. One day she found the courage to give him a choice: leave the army or she would leave him. He left the army and, for a while, living elsewhere, with Geordie driving long distance lorries, brought a kind of normality they had not known for years. Eventually, however, the old behaviours emerged. Geordie resented the hours; the money was not great. The arguments would start and so would the violence. Geordie announced one day that he was giving up the driving and opening a transport caff. He was going to be free and he was going to make some big money. After a couple of months, the cycle started again.

ABSOLUTION

Last night's beating had been the last. The children, at eighteen and nineteen, were old enough to look after themselves, as she did at their age. She was off and she was not coming back.

She breathed a sigh of relief. The sun broke through and fringed the clouds with a silver haze. She was going to find some peace; she was going to find herself; she was going to her sister's in Dagenham.

.

13

The streets were becoming busy with Saturday shoppers as Wyatt and Alice walked slowly back to the presbytery to collect his car.

Father Wyatt continued to offer soothing comfort as Alice gave direction. Within about twenty minutes they pulled into Bullpit Lane. The flat at number 15a had been converted in the nineteen-eighties as one of two from a nineteenth century semi-detached substantial town house. To the side was a small gravel drive leading to an imposing front door which gave access to the two flats. 15a was on the ground floor.

"Let me," said Wyatt, gently taking the key from Alice's hand.

Wyatt opened the door and entered. The first impression was of size and space; the second was of taste and style. In the centre of the room were two comfortable settees either side of a square heavy-legged glass-topped coffee table; at the tall windows hung rich red Roman blinds. In one corner stood a standard lamp with a Tiffany-style shade; in another a large television. Two low full bookshelves were set against adjacent walls over which hung abstract paintings of colourful squares, circles and lines.

"The kitchen is to the right," said Alice, breathing in fits and starts.

Wyatt nervously pushed open the door upon a large modern, dining kitchen. He was expecting to see a corpse on the floor. Instead, what he saw was a cast-iron frying pan face down on the marble-effect ceramic tiles and a smear of blood from his feet to the hob.

"There's nobody here," exclaimed Wyatt turning to Alice. "I mean, literally, no body." He emphasised the two words.

Alice pushed past him. "No, it can't be. I left him dead. I killed him. I know I did." Alice shook her head in disbelief, her eyes first staring at the floor, then darting round the kitchen, trying to find something that wasn't there.

"Let's check the other rooms," said Wyatt. "He may still be here lying injured." Wyatt left Alice the kitchen. "There's no one here," he said, on returning.

"But that just cannot be," insisted Alice.

"Let's think about this," said Wyatt, trying to make sense of it. He began, "There is the frying pan and there is blood. You hit him, he fell and you ran."

"Yes, but..." Alice tried to intervene.

"But Alice, there is no body," emphasised Wyatt. "So what is logical is that you hit him, but you didn't kill him. After you left, he got up and left. That would explain the blood smears on the floor. He may have gone to the hospital; he may have gone to a friend's. Does he have a car?"

"Yes, the car. Of course, the car. It's not on the drive. I didn't see it on the street. That's it. He's taken the car. He's gone somewhere." Relief showed on her face, tears welled.

Wyatt tried to take her in his arms but the movement was clumsy and she broke away as a new thought struck her.

"What if he comes back, Tom? I'm scared."

"I said I would help, and I will," said Wyatt, taking out his mobile and tapping in a number.

Alice looked apprehensive and quizzical.

"Extension 34, Diocesan Support, please," said Wyatt, then a moment later, "Good morning. Is that Sister Angela? Ah, Sister, Father Wyatt here. St. Jude's. Something unexpected has come up. As you know, my mother lives in Carlisle and she is not well. I don't like to ask at such short notice but I wonder if I might have a few days off."

Alice looked surprised.

"Yes, thank you Sister. Father Michael from Oxford. Yes, I know him. A good man. From this evening for ten days? Thank you again, Sister. I'll be going now." Wyatt ended the call.

Alice looked at him squarely, "Father, did you just tell a lie?"

"No Alice. I didn't. Everything I said was true.

Something unexpected has arisen, my mother does live in Carlisle and she is suffering from a mild chest infection. I didn't join the dots. Sister Angela did."

Alice looked at him searching his eyes for truth, confidence and certainty. She saw determination.

"Thanks, Tom," she said.

"And now," said Wyatt, "I must go and get some things. I'll be back within the hour. Bolt the door after I've gone and don't open it to anyone."

Alice locked and chained the door behind him and turned to the kitchen. She had some serious cleaning to do.

.

14

On the way to her car Kate phoned Sheldon to tell him that Ritchie Goodwin was dead, that they were now investigating a murder and that she would meet him outside The Black Cat about an hour later. She had first to make a quick visit.

That visit was to Laurel Close. The visit grated with Kate. How could you balance a murder against the disappearance of a cat? She knew though that if Mrs. Thompson was not given due attention then that very minor issue would grow and fester as a minor sore might develop sepsis. And a sepsis with the name of Fordyce was a very nasty complaint indeed.

Laurel Close was looking tidy, even hopeful. Neat front gardens sported snowdrops and the wide green verges were sprouting shoots. Within a couple of months the daffodils would be in full bloom, their yellow heads dancing in the April breezes.

Kate pressed the doorbell; the first few bars of **Jerusalem** sounded in the hall; a moment later the door opened.

"Mrs. Thompson, Inspector Kate Brown", said Kate, flashing her ID. "I've come about your cat."

Kate looked at the drawn and anxious face of a woman in her early fifties. Great care had been taken with the application of oils and unguents, powders and pastes.

There had been some attempt at subtlety in the blending of colours with hair and eyes but the overall effect was of someone trying too hard and, to Kate, the make-up, like the eyes, was beginning to show the signs of someone about to crack.

Kate looked round the sitting room as Mrs. Thompson insisted on making a cup of tea. Darjeeling or Earl Grey was the choice. Kate chose the Darjeeling. The room was comfortable, if over-padded, with soft furnishings but Kate's gaze was drawn to the French windows.

"Nice garden," she said, as Mrs. Thompson placed a tray on the glass-topped coffee table.

"Yes, my pride and joy. Let me show you."

"Not now Mrs. Thompson. I'm here about your cat. What can you tell me?" Kate asked, notebook and pen in hand. Marmalade is a ginger cat, but not any ordinary ginger. He is an Egyptian Mau – that's spelled M-A-U – a rare breed," said Mrs. Thompson with a nod of pride.

"How long has it...he..." corrected Kate before Mrs. Thompson could intervene, "been missing?"

"Over four days. He's a house cat. He doesn't go further than the garden. My neighbour told me of a gang of catnappers. Marmalade is valuable, not only as my companion, I've had him eight years, but in himself. If I had to replace him, but he is irreplaceable you understand, then it would cost us a great deal of money."

Kate's notes were swiftly jotted. "I have to tell you Mrs. Thompson that I am not aware of any gang of catnappers roaming the area. There have been no other reported thefts. I noticed on the lamp post outside that there was a poster. That's exactly the right thing to do. Local residents are likely to be the most help. However, I shall make sure the loss is logged, but do be sure to tell us if Marmalade turns up. A lovely garden," concluded Kate, rising to leave.

Pride once again flickered across Mrs. Thompson's face. "Thank you Inspector. Give my regards to Superintendent Fordyce when you see him."

"He'll be the first to be informed of progress," said Kate, masking the sarcasm with pretended sincerity. "He may even be in touch with you himself."

Kate followed Mrs. Thompson into the hall. As they were passing the stairs, Lee Thompson was descending.

"Lee," said Mrs. Thompson. "This is Inspector Brown. Do say hello. She's here to see about Marmalade."

Lee looked quickly at Kate and then at his mother. Pushing between them, he said with venom," Oh mother. You are priceless." And with that abruptly left the house.

Mrs. Thompson, as though teetering on the edge of a cliff, managed to control her breath. "I'm sorry about that Inspector. He's such a good boy really."

That was the second time that day Kate had heard a mother describe a son in such terms.

.

15

It is not without good reason The Cotswolds is designated an area of outstanding natural beauty. On its western side, a steep, wooded limestone escarpment dominated the expansive vales below. Heading east, minor roads criss-crossed, flanked by dry stone walls penning sheep or pasture. Man had settled here for millennia finding water, fertile land and defensible hills. He had built places to worship and places to bury the dead. Later, the Romans built huge villas at the heads of soft valleys. Later again, cottages with stone slates or thatch were built to house those that worked the land or tended the livestock while the landowners lived in extensive piles surrounded by parkland.

When the railway came, the land was cut and dug, carved and gouged but when the railway left about a hundred years later, nature began to reclaim what it could and a new kind of beauty was formed. The ancient trackways and deserted railway lines, the bridleways and the footpaths, the woods and streams, the hills and valleys, the thatched cottages, stone walls and chocolate box villages were redolent of a Golden Age, a time of hope, peace, freedom, comfort and security, a time when God was in his heaven and all was right with the world.

It is a desirable place to live and if you aren't lucky enough to have been born into it, you can buy into it at a price. The larger villages thrive as working or commuting communities; the smaller ones are full of second homes and only come alive at weekends and holidays. But you don't have to live in it or own it to enjoy its pleasures and surprises, to discover its secrets or to feel its restorative powers.

16

To Paul Levinson, manager of The Black Cat night club, Brett Barron was becoming a liability. Barron had been a useful conduit through which to shift the cocaine. Managing a car business, travelling up and down the country to car auctions or simply shifting stock had provided the perfect means of distribution. Levinson set up the contacts, Barron made the deliveries for which he was well paid and for which he actually had to do very little: take a parcel there, bring a parcel back. No questions. Easy.

Barron had been in The Black Cat on Thursday, drinking too much and stoned. Levinson approached him and, as to a customer, said, "Might I have a word sir?"

Barron released his arm from around the big-breasted brunette sitting next to him and stood up. "Sir," he guffawed. "Quite right. Call me sir. And what word would that be, mate," almost spitting out the last word at Levinson.

"Let's talk in private," said Levinson.

In a corridor at the back of the club, Levinson turned, pushed his forearm hard against Barron's throat and pinned him to the wall. "You're getting loud and loose, Barron. You're flashing the cash. You're sampling the goods. You're putting me and my business at risk. And I don't take unnecessary risks."

"Is that a threat?" uttered Barron, struggling for breath, unable to free himself.

"Just a warning, my friend, at the moment. Get yourself under control. I give only one warning."

Levinson released the pressure and stepped back. Barron tried to hold the gaze but dropped his head and spat on the floor before shaking himself down and heading back to the woman.

Barron was at the club again the following evening, larging it, this time with a trimmer black-haired girl. Levinson and Barron exchanged glances. Barron waved a wad of cash and asked a passing waitress for a bottle of champagne. Levinson nodded. The unspoken challenge was accepted.

Levinson looked at his watch. Nearly ten o'clock. Just then there was a commotion at the door and Levinson was called to deal with the stabbing of Ritchie Goodwin. It was going to be a busy night but Levinson smiled to himself. His real work was going to start after the club had closed.

After the police had gone and the last customer had left, Levinson drove round to Bullpit Lane and parked a few doors away from the flat at 15a. He took out his mobile and was starting to tap in Barron's number when he glanced up to see a blonde woman, mid-thirties, he guessed, dazed and stumbling leaving the flat. She looked as though she wasn't coming back.

Levinson completed the dialling. No answer but a redirection to a voicemail. Levinson left his car, checked there was nobody about and reached the front door. It was open; the lights were on. Carefully, he made his way through the lounge. At the kitchen, he stumbled against an arm. Barron was lying face down, prostrate, on the tiles, a small pool of blood forming beside his head. By his shoulder was a heavy duty frying pan.

Instinctively, he knelt down and felt for the pulse in Barron's neck. Nothing. Not the slightest movement. He turned the face. The eyes were dimming; no breath stirred. Barron was dead. Definitely dead. A scenario played out in Levinson's mind. Sure, the blonde woman would be held responsible, but the police and maybe her defence would want to look into Barron's background, behaviour and contacts. If they did their job thoroughly they would find their way to Town and Country Motors, then through Stevens to The Black Cat to Levinson. Levinson imagined a future about to implode.

A bold thought flashed brightly: a missing person is better than a dead body. Hot upon the thought, a plan, crystal clear, took shape. There were risks but in the early hours they were minimal, and if all went accordingly, Levinson would be back to see Stevens as planned.

Levinson picked up the car keys that were on the kitchen table. With effort he dragged the body along the hall, out through the door and into the back seat of the Toyota Rav 4 standing on the drive. That was the difficult bit, thought Levinson, panting. The rest is plain sailing.

Levinson knew of the tunnel from his childhood. A

few hills and valleys proved no obstacle to the Victorian engineers and entrepreneurs who with detailed plans, a lot of money and a gang of five thousand navvies carved their way into hillsides and spanned valleys. With the railway long gone the tunnel became for young adventurers a place of mystery, of darkness, an other world where danger and excitement lurked.

The tunnel was approached along a single line cutting. Tall trees, blanking out the sun, towered on either side; thick moss grew on tumbled stones; the air was heavy with damp, even in the height of summer. It was a magical and transformative place. The tunnel itself had been crudely blocked with breeze blocks into which an iron padlocked door had been set. Over the years, bigger kids, one supposed, had chipped and pulled, forced and bent, so that by the time the young Levinson had discovered it, the tunnel could be accessed.

There were puddles underfoot; water dripped and echoed. After five metres all light seemed to go. Reason told you that if you kept going you would come out the end into brightness; the imagination told you that you were entering an eternal blackness in which the walls whispered threats of collapse and perpetual entombment.

The young Levinson dared himself to go further and further until, about three hundred metres in, the tiniest flicker of light caught the dampness on the brick lining. At the same time, a draught of cold air touched the face like blind man's fingers. In two more steps he saw a pinprick of light ahead. His spirits lifted, and with the light becoming ever larger and brighter he walked confidently to the gaping mouth of the tunnel's exit. At this end, the breeze blocks lay in tumbled array; rusted beer cans and old litter mixed with the ashes of fires long since extinguished.

Over time, Levinson explored further. He traced above ground the half-mile length of the tunnel, and about half way along, to the side of a field, hidden in undergrowth, he found the shaft which brought the cold, damp air into the tunnel. The shaft was open like a well but well hidden amongst the brambles and trees. Levinson found a stone, dropped it into the shaft and a few seconds later heard the crack, echo and splash as the stone hit rough ground below.

In later years when passing, Levinson would occasionally stop and walk along the cutting to the tunnel's entrance. Time stood still in this green, damp, overgrown, alien, other world. Memories of childhood would flood back – memories of cruelty, fear, isolation and rejection – but here, in this cutting, at this tunnel's entrance, memories of excitement, adventure, mystery and magic. The only thing that had changed over the years was that both the tunnel's entrances had been re-blocked in double skin breeze blocks. Small gaps had been left near the tops of the arches to allow access for bats, birds and other creatures. There was little chance of future explorers getting into the tunnel. It became for Levinson the perfect hiding place, the ideal tomb. There was only one way in, and no way out.

Levinson heaved Barron's body over his shoulder and made his way along the top of the cutting at the field's edge then through the trees and brambles to the airshaft. The brambles resisted, caught and scratched but within a few minutes, Barron's head rested over the shaft. A push, a heave, a shove and the body slipped, slowly at first, then suddenly disappeared into the darkness below. Levinson heard the splash and the echoing thud. He smiled wryly to himself and repeated the thought: a missing person is better than a dead body, any day.

With the riskiest and most difficult part over, Levinson smiled and relaxed. The next steps were easy. In less than two hours he had driven the Rav 4 to the south coast. A mile or so east of Boscombe Pier, adjacent to the cliffside drive are numerous leafy streets. In summer, these streets are packed with parked cars, some belonging to residents but most to holiday makers or day trippers there to enjoy the golden sands. The parking then is metered and strictly enforced. In the winter, however, there are no restrictions. There is plenty of space to park and no one to check. The perfect place to hide a car is in plain view amongst other cars. It would be Easter before a traffic warden issued a ticket, and a good time after that before anyone would want to trace the owner.

Levinson locked the car. At the cliff top, beside the sign Danger. **Unstable Cliff. Keep Out** he flicked the key fob over the fence into the thickness of the gorse below. The morning was still on the edge of darkness. Nothing was stirring. Then imperceptibly the sky began to crack and spill out the palest of light onto Levinson's back as he headed to the town centre and the train station beyond.

17

Alice saw the car drive up and watched as Wyatt approached the door. Without a black suit and dog collar, Wyatt looked a different person. He seemed younger, and though not in the height of fashion with a red tartan lumberjack shirt, grey fleece jacket, jeans and heavy shoes, he did have a confident and attractive air.

Alice too looked different: her hair swept back and held in a loose bun; sweater jeans and yellow cleaning gloves which stopped just short of her elbows.

"I've nearly finished," she said.

To Wyatt, the kitchen gleamed. The floor looked spotless; the cupboards, appliances and radiators had all been cleaned from the tiles up.

"I've done this twice over," she continued, a note of pride in the voice.

"Well, it doesn't look like a crime scene now," replied Wyatt. He'd intended to be light-hearted, but Alice's face darkened, her shoulders sagged.

"I am covering up a crime. I'm confirming my guilt. I shouldn't have gone to you. I should have gone to the police." She looked pleadingly, almost despairingly, at Wyatt. "What am I supposed to do now?"

"Alice," Wyatt replied, "I'm sorry. That was clumsy of me. But there is no crime, because there is no body. Also an abused woman hitting her abusive partner is hardly the most serious matter. To the police this would be seen as a small domestic squabble. They would listen, of course, but what could they do? They might want to speak to...What is his name, by the way? I don't think you told me."

"Brett...Brett Barron."

"Brett...They may want to speak to Brett, but where is he? And as this is a first complaint I think the police might just thank you for having the courage to report. They would make a note, put it on file and ask you to report any further incidents."

"But Tom you're not hearing me. I'm not making a complaint. I'm making a confession. I'm sure I killed him."

For answer, Wyatt said, "Alice, we need to think about this more. Let's leave the flat for a while. Let's go somewhere we can get some fresh air and think through what's to be done."

About an hour later, mid afternoon as the sky was beginning to darken and the feeling of frost was in the air, Alice and Wyatt walked from the car park to the top of The Ridgeway.

The high ancient trackway afforded distant views, keen air and a preternatural spirituality. The evidence of people having lived, died and worshipped here was embedded in the soil and diffused in the vastness of the sky. It was a place where one could open the mind, clear thoughts and find perspective.

Alice and Wyatt walked side by side, two feet apart,

hands in pockets.

Wyatt began, "Tell me, what do you do for a living?"

"Oh, I'm a teacher. Secondary school. English. Lakeside Comprehensive. I've been there just over five years."

"You must find it rewarding."

"Like a priest. They are both what some people call vocations." Alice smiled, beginning to relax.

"Yes," said Wyatt. "Sometimes that's a word for a low-paid profession. If you're called to do it, you're not motivated by pay."

"That's a very useful lever politicians have been using for ever to keep down public sector pay. Completely unfair of course. But you, Tom, there's no money in being a priest so why do you do it?"

"Well, I did feel a yearning to want to help, to serve in some way, and in my idealistic teens, the highest, most noble way of doing that was to be a priest."

Alice nodded. "And is that what you feel now?"

Wyatt turned to her and smiled. "I still want to help and I'm here to serve in any way to help you through this."

For a moment, their eyes locked, then Wyatt turned away and pointed. "Look, the iron age fort. We can just get there and back before it gets dark."

Night was drawing in as they walked down the slope to

the car. Overhead the last of the rooks cawed their evening farewells.

Wyatt turned to Alice. "Brett has gone. We don't know if he's coming back. His things are still at your place so he might well do that. We don't know what state or mood he'll be in."

Alice took a breath. "Tom, would you stay over. At least tonight till we know what has happened."

"Of course. If I need to I could sleep on the sofa."

"That's all I've got," said Alice primly, in case there was any doubt.

"Yes. I meant if Brett came back, I wouldn't need to stay," flustered Wyatt and to recover himself said a little too quickly, "It's too early to go back. How about I treat you to dinner?"

"To dinner? That's a first," said Alice relaxing.

"It can't be the first time you've eaten out somewhere," said Wyatt.

"It is with a priest," smiled Alice, as she got into the car. "I'll pay."

.

18

He knew it was going to be tight but Levinson was still in time to get to Highfield by 11a.m. for his meeting with George Stevens, entrepreneur and owner of The Black Cat. Levinson had phoned him the previous evening to tell him of the stabbing. Stevens would have wanted to know in any case but, as the victim was his protégé, it was doubly important to tell him.

George Stevens, or Georgiou Stephanopoulou, as he was named at birth, was a self-made man several times over. Perhaps it was because he was brought up in England, the son of a Greek Cypriot father and a Northern Irish mother that he first became aware that he could be many people and do many things. He had, legitimately, three passports. These gave options. And he liked options. Like in business.

He learnt very early that the old cliché was true: it wasn't what you knew, though he knew a lot, but it was who you knew, and who you knew with money, that really counted. His Mediterranean good looks and his blarney won him backers, and when he was able to show good returns he was backed even more. He hadn't had to take too many short cuts or cut too many corners. He was good at what he did; he could read markets and trends and he spread his risks. He repaid his debts; he grew in wealth and influence.

He considered himself a man of honesty and integrity but he knew also that to keep everything as he wanted, to remain in control, he had to be vigilant and to have the right people around him.

He prided himself on his ability to judge character and in Ritchie Goodwin he recognised something of himself, someone who was honest, solid, bright, insightful, hard working, articulate, and charismatic. Ritchie was the son he didn't, indeed couldn't, have, his spiritual heir being groomed for greatness.

In Levinson he saw clarity, order, strength, decisiveness and loyalty. Levinson brought solutions not problems, and was well rewarded for his talents. The Black Cat night club was a smooth-running, money-making machine. It was a cash business with no leakages. Stevens liked that. It was well run; there was no trouble ever big enough to cause embarrassment to Stevens in his standing in the community. Stevens liked that too.

Levinson was a man on whom he could depend, so when Stevens got the call the previous evening, he was doubly disturbed, first by the violence, then by the victim. He arranged for Levinson to see him at home Saturday 11 a.m. for a full account.

Highfield, solid and Georgian, sat squatly at the head of a wooded valley and was approached by a long avenue double-lined with trees. Cherry trees stood like pawns guarding their chestnut tree kings. The sward either side merged with pasture on which sheep grazed.

As Levinson tapped in the gate number and rolled gently over the cattle grid he reconfirmed to himself where his ambitions lay. He would own this or something like it before too long.

Except for his staff, Stevens, until recently, lived alone at Highfield. Not that there hadn't been, and continued to be, many opportunities to change that but, as in business so in his personal life, Stevens valued loyalty and fidelity. When his wife died twenty years before of leukaemia, he accepted, indeed determined, there would be no other. He continued to be open, social, friendly warm and generous. He took mistresses when he needed too; he had dates and female companions, but none was permitted to stay long in his house, nor in his heart, though that was beginning to change.

Stevens was sitting at his desk when Levinson was shown in.

"Dreadful business Paul," Stevens began indicating that Levinson should take the seat opposite. "You look exhausted as though you've been up all night. Tell me what you know."

Levinson sat down, rubbed his temples, palmed the tiredness from his face and began. "About ten, there was a disturbance outside. I was called to find Ritchie had been stabbed. Police and ambulance were called. Ritchie was taken to hospital where I understand he is still in intensive care."

"Do you know who did it and why?" questioned Stevens.

"No idea. The police are looking into it. They checked the CCTV but there were no clear images. No one in the queue seemed to see any one. It's early days yet."

"I still don't understand why," said Stevens. "He's a good lad, smart, hard working, never in trouble, though he did tell me last week there was something he was a little worried about and he'd like to talk over but he wanted to be sure first. No idea what, but it didn't seem urgent. This stabbing just seems so random."

"It's a mystery," said Levinson looking concerned, "but I'm sure the police will get some answers soon."

"Let's hope so. I'll contact Fordyce, Superintendent Fordyce. I know him well. In the meantime get some rest. It's Saturday. The club is open again tonight. Keep me posted." Stevens nodded to indicate the interview was over.

Back in his car, heading down the drive, Levinson palmed his face once more and thought: Georgie boy's going to have another mystery on Monday when he finds out Barron hasn't turned up for work.

.

19

"This is now a murder investigation," said Inspector Kate Brown to Sergeant Joe Sheldon as they approached The Black Cat. "Let's hope the manager can give us more to go on."

"Yes ma'am."

The frontage looked dull in the coming gloom of late afternoon. The neon lights were not illuminated. Finding no bell or knocker, Kate pushed the bright red door which to her surprise opened. She stepped into the lobby. Beyond the cloakrooms the space opened out into a large square, wooden-floored area. It was dark. There were no windows. Without the bright lights, sounds and people, it felt to Kate more like walking into a large cave. As she became accustomed to the lack of light Kate could make out there was a long bar against the far wall. To each side were sets of alcoves with benches and tables each of which would seat eight or ten people. Above, there was a galleried landing supporting in one corner turntables and sound equipment, and what appeared to be another bar.

Their footsteps echoed as they crossed the hall to a door marked 'Private'. Kate knocked. A chair scraped. The door opened.

"Yes, Inspector," said Levinson. "How can I help?"

They sat on hard chairs in a triangular formation. Joe had his notebook out. Levinson sipped a coffee.

Kate began, "The first thing I have to say is that we are now investigating a murder. Ritchie Goodwin died of his wounds earlier today."

Levinson started, nearly tipping his coffee. "No, that cannot be."

"I'm afraid so. We'd like to find more about what happened and why it happened."

"I think I told you all I knew on Friday. I'm not sure if there's anything I can add," responded Levinson.

"I understand he was employed on the recommendation of a Mr. George Stevens," said Kate.

"Yes, that's right," replied Levinson. "Ritchie works...worked for Mr. Stevens as an office manager or something like that."

"And Mr. Stevens is?" continued Kate.

"You must have heard of Mr. Stevens. Businessman, wealthy, well-connected. He owns a number of businesses including this one."

Kate raised an eyebrow. Sheldon made a note.

"So you know Mr. Stevens well?"

"Yes. I saw him only the other day. He doesn't interfere on a day-to-day basis. As long as things are well run and the money adds up, he's happy to leave things to me. He's going to be upset when he hears about Ritchie."

"Upset?" queried Kate.

"Distraught then. Whatever." Kate made a mental note of the tetchiness in the reply. Levinson collected himself. " Mr. Stevens liked Ritchie. Treated him like a son. Some might say, indulged and spoilt him. I wouldn't say that of course. I hardly knew him. He's only been here a short time."

"And who might the 'some' be?" asked Kate, seizing the negativity in Levinson's answer.

"Oh, I suppose other people he worked with. I don't know really." Levinson shifted in his seat.

"So you know people in Mr. Stevens' other businesses," persisted Kate.

"I get to know a lot of people running a club like this. I must have picked up something somewhere. You know, just a hint, just a feeling." Levinson shifted position once more. "I'm not sure I can help you further. As I say, I hardly knew the boy."

Kate turned to Joe. "Anything you would like to ask, Sergeant?"

"Yes," said Joe, looking directly at Levinson. "We checked the CCTV cameras on Friday. Could we now take the tapes with us, just to make sure we didn't miss anything?"

"I'm sorry. That won't be possible. The tapes have been re-used."

Sheldon raised an eyebrow and glanced towards Kate.

"Re-used? Already? It's standard practice to keep tapes for at least a week. Often longer."

"That may be so, Sergeant, and we usually do, I hasten to add. It's just that we're short of them and, as the tapes had been checked, I thought it would be alright to re-use them."

"That's unfortunate," intervened Kate. "You look like you run a well-organised business here. A bit of an oversight then."

"These things happen," replied Levinson, holding Kate's gaze, and rubbing his palm against his cheek. "Well, if there's nothing else," he concluded, rising from his chair.

"Not for the moment, Mr. Levinson."

Outside, Kate turned to Sheldon. "What did you make of the business of the tapes?"

"A bit odd," replied Sheldon.

"Agreed. Also, I couldn't read his reaction to the news of Ritchie's death. Surprised? Shocked? Annoyed?"

"Maybe. I don't think he liked him, anyway," said Sheldon.

"Perhaps he was relieved then," said Kate.

.

20

That Sunday felt like a holiday to Father Wyatt. As he was washing the dishes after breakfast, he began whistling chirpily. At this time, he thought, I would be celebrating mass; the faithful would be at prayer. There would be afternoon visits to the sick and elderly to look forward to. But instead, I am sharing domestic duties with a ... He left the thought uncompleted, suddenly shocked, empty of courage.

Alice said, "Tom, I have to go to school tomorrow. I can't just take the time off. It'll help me take my mind off things."

"I'll stay and look after the flat in case Brett comes back."

"If he doesn't, is he a missing person?" queried Alice. "Should I report him to the police as missing?"

"A day or two is much too soon for that," replied Wyatt. "Different if it's a child, but an adult, they would send you home to wait. But what I could do," continued Wyatt, "is to go to his workplace and see if he's there. That way, we may be able to find out where he's staying and what mood he's in."

.

21

Wyatt tried to have a plan in mind when he left the flat just after ten on the Monday morning, but plans rely on projections from fixed points, from clear expectations rather than vague hopes, so it was with a mixture of unease and determination that he made his way across town to Town and Country Motors on Orleans Way.

Set amongst some large car franchises and furniture outlet stores, Town and Country Motors made a bold statement. On the verge fronting the road stood a white 1954 Rolls Royce Silver Dawn at an angle. Adjacent to it, mirroring the angle stood a blue 1960 Bentley S2 and between them facing straight onto the road was a red 1968 Mark 1 Austin Mini. All of them gleaming; all of them in perfect condition; all of them not for sale.

Behind them on the concourse was a more modest selection of second hand cars, none more than five years old. SUVs and hatchbacks nestled side by side with estates and coupés. If you were in the market for a car and had the money you would be spoilt for choice. Even on a winter's day the cars exuded desire like temptresses: try me, buy me, they seemed to whisper.

Wyatt avoided the temptation and entered the reception. The first impression was welcoming: fresh cut flowers stood in a vase on a coffee table which was flanked by two easy chairs. Against the adjacent wall was a coffee machine with a 'Please help yourself' sign. On another wall were a number of framed certificates and a photograph of smiling personnel. There was a counter in front with a desk pad and pen set, and a bowl of mint imperials.

Behind the counter, a woman, mid-forties, chubby but fragrant was just returning the phone to its cradle.

"Good morning," she said. "I'm Sharon. How may I help?"

"Good morning," said Wyatt, "I'm here to see Mr. Barron."

"Do you have an appointment?" Sharon replied tapping a keyboard and glancing at a screen.

"No, I'm calling in on the off chance," Wyatt replied.

"Well, I'm afraid you can't see him at the moment. He hasn't arrived and I'm not sure when to expect him. Can anyone else help?"

"No, I don't think so," said Wyatt.

"I could book an appointment for you. Tomorrow perhaps?"

No, that won't be necessary, thank you. But I wonder if you might give me his contact details."

"I can give you his business card but I'm not at liberty to give any other personal details."

"The card would be fine, thanks."

Sharon fished in a drawer and handed a card over.

"I'm surprised you don't have one of these already. He tends to shower them on people like confetti," said Sharon attempting a chuckle which, to Wyatt, resembled the braying of an ass.

"I'll try these numbers," said Wyatt glancing at the card, "but rather than keep troubling the office would you contact me when he comes in?"

Wyatt picked up the desk pen and note pad, wrote down his contact details, tore off the sheet and put it into Sharon's outstretched hand.

"It would be my pleasure, Mr Wyatt," replied Sharon, glancing at the note. "Would you like a coffee before you go?"

"No, that's very kind. I must be off."

"Then do at least take a mint imperial," said Sharon offering the bowl.

Feeling obliged, Wyatt took two, popped them into his mouth, nodded his thanks and left.

To the right was a workshop, shutters fully open to the winter chill. Two mechanics were working, one head buried deep in the engine bay of an Mercedes, the other changing a wheel of a black SUV. The mechanic at the Mercedes looked up. "Yes, mate. What do you want?"

The tone was not unfriendly. He was probably in his fifties, slim with thin greying hair. His overalls were cleaner than Wyatt might have expected. He wore green disposable gloves. He looked more like a surgeon performing a delicate operation rather than a mechanic. He looked professional, skilled; someone you could trust to do a good job.

"I was looking for Brett Barron," said Wyatt.

"You won't find him here," the mechanic replied. "Doesn't know much about the inside of a car. Try the office."

"I have," said Wyatt. "I was told he hasn't come in yet."

"No real surprise there. Flexihours, I think he calls it. He's done a lot of that recently. He's not that flexi when he wants a car done urgently, mind. This one's supposed to be ready by midday so he can deliver it to a customer, so if you don't mind, mate, I'll get on," said the mechanic turning back to the car.

"No, of course not. Thank you," said Wyatt, then taking a chance as an afterthought, "You wouldn't know where he lives. I've something important to see him about."

"Bullpit Lane. About half way down. I dropped him there once. The office will give you the address."

I don't think they will, thought Wyatt, as he nodded his thanks to the mechanic and walked away.

Before he drove off, Wyatt took a moment to reflect: Barron was expected at work, even needed to be there. He hasn't let them know. No one yet seems particularly worried. No one's tried to contact him. Wyatt took out his mobile and the business card, took a deep breath and tapped in Barron's number. The phone rang until it was diverted to voicemail. Wyatt ended the call. So, not at work, no answer on his mobile. The blood on the kitchen floor suggested an injury, probably not serious. Wyatt tried to think what he might do in such circumstances. Would he go to the hospital or to a friend's house? In the early hours of the morning that wouldn't be an easy choice but a friend would be more understanding; there would be less formality; nothing on record. But then it would depend on how serious the injury was. Also, he didn't know any of Barron's friends but he did know where the hospital was.

It was quiet in Accident and Emergency. There were two patients waiting: an older man with an ashen face, and a teenager clutching an arm.

The nurse on reception was Mrs. McNally. Wyatt knew her and approached her breezily. "Nurse McNally, how lovely to see you. All well I hope."

"Why, Father Wyatt, what a surprise! I nearly didn't recognise you without you dog collar," she said, her broad Irish face breaking into a smile. "I thought you were away."

"I have a few days off to ..."

"...see your mother," completed Mrs. McNally. "I know. Father John mentioned it at mass yesterday. I thought you'd already gone."

"I'll be on my way soon," said Wyatt, smiling in return, "but before I go I just needed to check up on something.

Would you know if anyone reported in with a head injury, early hours Saturday morning?"

With an unquestionable faith in the authority of priests, Mrs. McNally turned to her computer screen, rolled the mouse. "Let me see. Saturday night, Sunday morning. Say between midnight and five. Are we looking for a male or female?"

"Male, late thirties early forties."

"Name?"

"Barron. Brett Barron."

Mrs. McNally studied the screen. "No, nothing Father. A car accident female; a cardiac arrest, older male. Quiet for a Saturday, and no Mr. Barron."

"Thank you Mrs. McNally."

"You're welcome, Father. All the best now to your mother for a speedy recovery."

"Thank you Mrs. McNally. God bless."

On the way back to his car, Wyatt wore a puzzled look. What next? was one thought. Am I beginning to lie? was another.

Over dinner that evening Wyatt described the fruitlessness of his day.

"Brett was expected at work, but no one seemed to mind too much, and I got the impression he could come and go pretty much as he pleased."

"He didn't tell me too much about his work, though I know his hours were irregular because of delivering cars," added Alice. "When he was late I used to worry about whether there had been an accident. When I realised lateness was because he was out socialising with other women then things began to turn sour." Alice's lips began to twist with bitterness.

To lighten the mood, Wyatt said, "I'm not much of a detective, I'm afraid. All I got for my efforts were two mint imperials and this." He took the business card form his pocket and passed it over to Alice. "I tried the number," continued Wyatt. "No answer, just a direction to voice mail."

"Try it again," urged Alice nervously. "I can't. I daren't."

Wyatt took out his mobile and tapped in the number. The faintest of rings could be heard from the bedroom.

Alice started, "No, it can't be!" She ran to the bedroom and returned, looking disbelievingly at the phone in her hand.

The ringing stopped.

Alice looked at Wyatt, "This can't be. There's something wrong. Brett never ever leaves without his phone."

"He'd received a knock on the head. Perhaps he just left quickly to find help. He could drive okay. He's probably resting up somewhere, and when he feels better he'll return," suggested Wyatt.

Alice shook her head in doubt.

Suddenly inspired, Wyatt said, "We have his phone so we have his contact list. Why don't we go through it and see who answers. We could say we're trying to contact Brett to return his phone and would they know where he is."

Alice nodded uncertainly. "I don't like to pry. It feels wrong somehow like reading someone's diary or stealing money from a friend's wallet."

"I don't see what alternative we have," said Wyatt. "We could hang on to it for a few days and give it to the police. But what would they do? If he doesn't come back they would probably do the same, just go through the contacts and see what turns up."

Alice nodded in resignation, handing over the phone. "Okay Tom, but you do it. I'm not sure I want to know who he's been dealing with."

Tom swiped the green button, bringing up the keypad. Underneath were the links to recent calls and contacts. Tom pressed the contact link. A list appeared. Tom scrolled up and down. "Hey, that's odd," he said. "Look at this Alice. There are no names as such, only single words. None of them look like surnames. Just random words like a code, and not many of them either."

Alice leaned over his shoulder. "Weird," she said. "Looks like he's got something to hide. Maybe he has another phone."

"He would have your number surely, Alice. Let's first

go through the numbers and see if we can find you."

Seconds later, Alice exclaimed, "Hey, stop. That's mine. Imp. Imp?"

"Imp? What's that? Little devil? Short for imperial? Important? Impossible?" Wyatt smiled.

Alice took the comment good-humouredly and pushed his shoulder affectionately.

"I know," she said. "It's a link to my surname. Green. Lincoln Green. Lincoln Imp. Imp."

"Sounds plausible," said Wyatt. Perhaps all the others are are connected through association or wordplay. There are nineteen other names, beginning with Anchor and ending with Winkle."

"Anchor?" mused Alice.

"Crown and Anchor," suggested Wyatt, "or maybe rhyming slang for an unsavoury person?"

Alice laughed, "Father Tom, surely you don't know such words!"

"Oh, I know them alright," he replied. "I don't use them though. Well not often anyway."

They looked at each other and laughed. She left her hand on his shoulder as he tapped the number.

22

The last time George Stevens was left so shaken was when his wife passed away twenty years before. Then the loss was huge, but it was expected. The pain was not diminished but he could come to terms with illness: unfair, unjust perhaps, but part of a natural order. When he put down the phone after being told of Ritchie's death he was numbed into inaction. He grew pale, sat and stared. He was jolted out of his shock by the ringing of the phone. He picked it up mechanically.

"Sorry to trouble you, Mr. Stevens. Sharon here, Town and Country Motors. I didn't know who to call. You see, Mr. Barron didn't turn up today, and I wondered if you knew where he was."

"Have you tried his phone? His home?" responded Stevens lethargically.

"I tried to call him several times, but no answer. I suppose I could call at his place on my way home," Sharon said doubtfully," but I've had several people wanting him and there are some cars ready for delivery. I am sorry to trouble you with this."

"You've done the right thing, Sharon. Leave it with me. If he doesn't turn up tomorrow morning, let me know," said Stevens replacing the phone abruptly.

Stevens sat back as though exhausted but the emotions running through him were hard to define. He was shocked and saddened, certainly, but the overriding emotion was of being unsettled. The old certainties were under threat. The ground was beginning to rumble; the edifice was beginning to shake; cracks were beginning to appear. He felt he had to get a grip somehow, to establish control. But what use is a banister when the staircase is collapsing?

He shook himself out of his reverie and tried to find perspective: an unexpected death and an employee that doesn't turn up for work. That is hardly the end, or the beginning of the end, he said to himself. He picked up the phone, tapped and asked to be put through to Superintendent Fordyce.

23

Kate and Joe were at their desks typing up progress reports and planning next steps when Fordyce called them into his office.

"Inspector Brown, Sergeant Sheldon. A serious business this assault... murder. I've just been speaking to the lad's employer, friend of mine, George Stevens. Terribly upset."

"His mother's upset too," said Kate.

"Yes, quite. Get to the bottom of this. Leave no stone unturned," ordered Fordyce. "Oh and before you go, George mentioned that one of his employees, Brett Barron, manager of Town and Country Motors, didn't turn up for work. Probably not important but I said you'd look into if he's not there tomorrow."

Kate was dumbfounded. "Sir, a murder and someone late for work. They don't quite equate." She looked in disbelief at Joe who raised his eyebrows and shrugged.

"As I said Inspector, probably not important, but all part of the same big family as it were. So bear it in mind and keep me updated on all fronts. That'll be all."

Kate turned away brusquely, keen to get out of the office.

"And Inspector. thank you for seeing Mrs. Thompson.

Her husband phoned to say she was very impressed with the attention you showed over her cat. Still missing but not to worry. The important thing is she feels attended to."

Kate hardly heard the last few words as she strode out of the Superintendent's office, leaving Joe to say, "Sir" and follow on softly behind.

24

Wyatt put the mobile on speaker phone so Alice could hear.

"The Anchor. How can I help?" sounded a male voice.

"I'm looking for Brett Barron," said Wyatt.

"Never heard of him, mate," came the reply.

"But I have this number. That is The Anchor...pub," guessed Wyatt, "in...Where exactly are you?"

"Bristol, mate. What is this? Some kind of scam?" the voice becoming more belligerent."

"No, I'm looking for my friend Brett." Wyatt tried to sound convincing about the use of the word 'friend'.

"Well I suggest you look elsewhere." The line went dead.

"That went well," said Wyatt looking at Alice. "Let's try the next one. Ah, Bitch. Are you sure you want to listen to this?"

"Bring it on," said Alice resignedly. "The more I'm finding out the more uncomfortable I feel, the darker this whole thing is becoming. But I know I've been betrayed, so nothing more is going to hurt or surprise me."

"Only if you're sure."

Alice nodded. Wyatt tapped the number. A squeaky female voice answered.

"Brett, darling. Where have you been? I've been waiting here wanting, desiring, no... lusting after your kind attentions but you never called. Couldn't you get away from that blonde cow you live with. Well, I'm here. I'm ready. I'm waiting..."

Wyatt ended the call without saying anything. Alice was tight-lipped and grim-faced.

"He's not there, anyway," said Wyatt. "I've blocked the number. We don't want her phoning back." He continued, "So the names are giving us people and places. No mystery with the pub. We probably know what he thinks of the last one. Let's try this one. Ozy."

After a couple of tones, a voice answered, "Brett! What on earth is going on?" The voice sounded warm, cultured.

"It's not Brett, Mr...." began Wyatt.

"Stevens. Who is this? And where's Brett?"

"I'm a friend of his partner. Brett seems to have gone missing. We're a little worried. He left his phone behind so we thought we would try his friends and contacts."

"If you manage to get hold of him, tell him I want to speak to him urgently," The line went dead.

"He doesn't know where he is either. Why Ozy though? Ozzy Osbourne? Black Sabbath?" pondered Wyatt.

"No I don't think so," the slightest of smiles appearing on Alice's face. "Too cultured. Maybe short for Ozymandias, the all-powerful ruler who thought his empire would never decay."

"How do you know that," said Wyatt, impressed.

"English teacher. We read a lot," replied Alice.

"Brett must have read too," added Wyatt.

"He might have been abusive and treacherous but he wasn't uneducated," replied Alice, a little too quickly, a little too sharply.

It might not have been intended but Wyatt suddenly felt deflated. He put the phone down. "That's enough for now," he said.

Alice turned and made her way to the bedroom.

.

25

Misha was excited when she heard the door open. She ran down the hall and flung her arms around Kate's waist.

"Wow! What a welcome," exclaimed Kate. "You're obviously much better," lifting up Misha and planting a big kiss on her cheek.

"Granny and I had such a lovely time. I baked a cake. Granny said we might have it before I go to bed. Can we Mummy?" pleaded Misha.

"I don't see why not," smiled Kate, "but not too late. You've got school tomorrow." Kate turned to her mother, "Thanks, Mum." Granny smiled. And then to Misha, "A little slice now, then bath and bed."

Misha collected the cake from the side and presented it proudly as though it was a crown for a coronation. Like a crown it was round and glittered, but that was where the comparison ended. The top of the cake was splodged with blobs of red and blue icing.

Kate looked a little quizzical. "These are..."

"Pansies, Mummy. Like we have in the garden."

"They're lovely," said Kate, taking a bite. "Delicious."

Misha beamed.

"I'll be off then," said Granny. "There's some dinner

in the oven. You look exhausted."

"Thanks, Mum. I am grateful. Perhaps I don't show it enough, but I am."

"I know it's been difficult since Martin died. Anytime you need me, just say," said Granny putting on her coat. She turned to leave, but hesitated and turned back. "Perhaps it's not the right time to say it, but have you thought about remarrying, or at least bringing another man into your life. You have a beautiful daughter there and a demanding job. Perhaps she needs a father figure, to feel part of a complete family, and perhaps you need support."

Kate looked at her mother, less with anger than exhaustion. "Mum, I am...we are her family. That's it. Nobody can replace Martin as father or husband and to think that somehow that would be possible is foolish. And even if I felt I needed to or wanted to have another man in my life, it just wouldn't work. He would always be second best. He would know it. I would know it. It would be a recipe for misery. So please, Mum, no more."

Granny shrugged. "Well it was just a thought. Give that little darling a hug from me," and with that she closed the door behind her.

The lasagne her mother had made was comforting; the glass of red wine she was drinking was soothing. As she looked at Martin's photograph, Kate was pensive. Captain Martin Brown of the 4th Gloucestershire Light Infantry, in full dress uniform, looked every inch the confident leader. To Kate he was friend, lover and husband; to Misha he was adoring father; to his friends he was the courageous team player with a warm sense of humour; to his men he was supportive, encouraging, clear and decisive. And to them all he was dead, killed in action in Afghanistan seven years before.

Kate had received the letters of condolence, mostly rather formulaic, though the one from his immediate commanding officer was more personal. They spoke of his honour, bravery, and leadership but even after a conversation with Major Hornton, Kate was still vague about the actual circumstances of his death.

From what she could gather, Martin was establishing a forward operating base, not a full blown encampment, but a small barbed wire affair, the first foothold in hostile territory. A couple of days in the wire was breached. There was gunfire. Martin and his translator were killed together with two insurgents. Those that remained were able to keep the insurgents at bay until reinforcements arrived.

The formalities were well observed: the dignified procession through Wootton Bassett, the cavalcade along the M5 to the full honours of a military burial, at Martin's request, at Brookwood.

When Kate had accepted the reality of his death and began to adjust to a new normality, she wanted to know more about the actual circumstances of the attack on the base, in particular why and how the defences had been breached. She met a wall of vagueness and platitudes. She wasn't sure whether the authorities were just embarrassed or had something to hide. In the void, suspicion arose. That suspicion nagged at her.

She had asked Major Hornton for the names of the other soldiers who were there, the first hand witnesses, but he would give nothing away, citing the Official Secrets Act. She had written officially to the Ministry of Defence, to the minister himself, but the replies spoke of Martin's courage, offered sympathy, were sorry for hers and the country's loss, but gave no details.

Sitting there, reflecting on Martin's death and the death of Ritchie Goodwin, she reconfirmed for herself one of her principal motivations for becoming a detective police officer. People wanted answers. Those affected wanted restoration and, if they couldn't have that, they wanted knowledge, truth and honesty; they wanted to understand, for understanding can bring acceptance, and with that a kind of peace. Understanding, too, can lead to a call for action, a desire for justice. As Kate drained the last of her wine and rose to go to bed she thought that there was probably a very fine line between a desire for justice and a thirst for revenge.

26

Kate was on the way to work that Tuesday morning when she received the call to divert her to the layby on the high road near Cotedge. An unspecified serious incident had been called in. Kate flicked on the blue flashing lights and put her foot down.

As she approached the scene she could see order trying to be made out of chaos. The layby was taped. Two uniformed officers about a hundred metres apart were controlling the traffic. Despite their frantic arm movements, the officers were unable to speed up the unnecessarily slow traffic. Kate weaved in and out. When she reached the first officer she flashed her ID and ordered, "Constable, when the next squad car arrives, block the road either end and set up a diversion. Then clear these rubberneckers as fast as you can."

"Yes, ma'am," came the reply.

An ambulance, door open, had already arrived and was close to the single-decker bus. A paramedic stood next to a uniformed constable. Inside the ambulance her colleague was attending to a middle aged man around whose shoulders was a blanket. He was ashen-faced and shaking.

Kate approached the constable, showed her ID and nodded to the paramedic.

"What do we have, officer?" began Kate.

"Dead male. Forties at a guess. Shot in the head."

Kate grimaced, "Who called it in and when?"

The officer replied, "The guy in the back of the ambulance, a Mr..." the officer looked at his notebook, "...Jonas Harbottle. About forty minutes ago. We got here about the same time as the ambulance nearly half an hour ago. There was a bit of a crowd. Constable Perkins over there is taking statements but it looks as though there were no witnesses. Harbottle was the first to arrive. He's shaken and hasn't given us anything yet. Scenes of crime and forensic pathologist are on their way."

"Thank you, officer. Good work. Looks as if they're starting to arrive," Kate said, as a large white van, lights flashing, emblazoned with *Crime Scene Investigation Unit*, pulled in alongside the ambulance.

The passenger descended and approached Kate. "Larry Holmes CSIU." He showed his ID as a formality.

"Old habits, eh, Sherlock," said Kate. "You show me yours but I'm not going to show you mine."

"Not for your benefit, Kate. But for his," said Larry nodding at the constable and smiling.

"If that's all, ma'am, I'll go help Perkins finish with that lot over there," said the constable, heading off to the far end of the layby.

"Well Kate, what have we got?" said Larry.

"I'm told a shooting. Male. We'll have to wait for Dr. Grant to check the body. I'll let you get on setting up and see if the guy who reported it is in a better state to chat. I'll see you shortly."

"Right. Better get dressed," said Larry, returning to the van where his colleague had already donned his white overalls and was beginning to erect a screen to mask the bus from the road.

Kate approached the ambulance. "Mr. Harbottle?" The man nodded. "Are you up to answering a few questions?" The man nodded again and pulled the foil blanket tighter around him. "What time did you get to the café?"

"Just after eight," Harbottle's voice wavered. "I stopped on the off chance."

"Never been here before then," asked Kate.

"No. I've been past a few times. It always looked a good place. Interesting. Clean. Just fancied a coffee before hitting the motorway."

"On the way to work?"

"Yes. Sales meeting in Bristol at ten. Plenty of time. Well there was. I need to make some calls," Harbottle said, suddenly touching his pockets to locate his phone.

"Soon, Mr. Harbottle, nearly finished. What did you see?"

"Nothing but the body. I went to the counter. The first thing I noticed was the bacon sizzling. I called out. Then I saw the broken window, the blood and then the body. I was shocked, I can tell you. I phoned 999 and that was it. A few other cars stopped and we waited for the police and ambulance."

"Did you see anyone leaving as you arrived? A car or motorbike, maybe a lorry or van? Perhaps even a bicycle or a pedestrian?"

"No nothing. The layby was empty. Nobody here."

"Thank you, Mr. Harbottle. The officer has taken your contact details?" Harbottle nodded. "We'll be in touch if we need to. You're free to go when you feel you're able to."

Kate was walking back to the bus as Dr. Grant, forensic pathologist, drew alongside her in a black Mercedes saloon.

"Inspector. A shooting, I'm told," said Dr. Grant crisply.

"Yes, doctor," returned Kate.

"Give me five minutes." It was an order not a request.

Kate nodded.

Dr. Grant struck an imposing figure, tall, thin, imperious. His grey hair was swept back from a gaunt, lined face dominated by a hooked nose. His eyes were piercing. In another life he could have been a Roman emperor or an eagle. He exuded control and authority, intelligence and precision. In less than five minutes he had put his blue coveralls over his tailored tweed suit, had slipped the plastic covers over his Oxford brogues and was making his way, bag in hand, on to the bus.

There was little room in the galley but Dr. Grant moved with ease and efficiency. Three minutes later he emerged.

"Inspector, my preliminary examination confirms a) the man is dead; b) he was shot; and c) he was shot no longer than two hours ago. Generally, I would say he is in his mid-forties, unfit, an occasional drug user with an underlying health condition, probably asthma. The autopsy will be more precise. Scenes of crime will tell you more but if I were a betting man, which I most certainly am not, my money would be on a professional slaying. You can move the body when you're ready. I will have a fuller report by lunch time tomorrow. Good day, Inspector," and almost as an afterthought, "and good luck."

"Thank you, doctor."

Kate beckoned to Larry. "Over to you now, Sherlock. The doc reckons foul play, maybe professional. I want everything checked with your usual thoroughness. Let me have all of the victim's personal effects as soon as you can. I'll take them straight to forensics and get the ball rolling. You can send the body off as soon as you've finished taking the photographs."

"Professional, eh?" said Larry. "That's nasty."

"Yes," said Kate. "I want to know who the victim is. But more importantly, I want to know why."

She gazed beyond the layby to the rolling hills, the copses and thickets and lush fields where the sheep were grazing the winter pasture. The pale sun was warming the dry stone walls; steam was rising in the freshness of the air; the year was on the turn.

This should be a place of restoration and renewal, Kate thought, not violent death.

27

Alice and Wyatt exchanged the briefest of greetings the next morning. It was as though an intangible heaviness had come between them. What had seemed so promising was, in the cold light of day, a realisation that they were in a hopeless situation.

Alice couldn't shake off the feeling that something was dreadfully wrong. Brett, she was convinced, was dead but she couldn't account for the lack of a corpse. She had tried to tell Tom but his rationality couldn't suppress her anxiety; and if she tried to tell him again, he would consider her neurotic, mad perhaps. And then there was Tom. What would drive a priest to follow her, to pretend to his superiors, to begin to lie? He was staying in her flat; they were sharing meals; they were behaving like friends, or even co-habitees to external onlookers, yet they hardly knew each other. She was also finding out more about Brett. Just the oddity of the names on the contacts list suggested a darker side than she had imagined. She knew he was dead but, at the same time, feared his return. Any affection she had for him had gone long before she had hit him. She wanted finality, completion. She wanted to escape the past but felt trapped. She wanted certainty. She wanted to be understood. Perhaps most of all she wanted forgiveness.

Wyatt, too, was conflicted. He always considered himself to be measured rather than spontaneous, reflective rather than impetuous, rational rather than emotional, and yet he had responded quite out of character in following

Alice, offering his help and taking time off. His duty of looking after a flock had become a desire to help just one person. The general had become particular, and desire was more than a vague wish or hope, it was becoming a controlling, almost all-encompassing, passion; and that passion was not just spiritual, it was physical. He was feeling something he had thought to be beyond him or had long suppressed, the feeling of wanting both to love and be loved, not in some vague, generalised, cosy, schmaltzy way but with an intensity he had never before thought or imagined: a dense fusion, a cosmic singularity of spirit, mind, body and soul.

"Thank you for that," said Alice as she put down her fork. "It was delicious and welcome."

"You can't beat a fridge-emptying stir fry," replied Wyatt. "It's not fine dining but interesting, nutritious, virtuous and the chance to start again." Realising the potential ambiguity, Wyatt added, "I meant restock the fridge."

Alice looked at him. He shuffled back his chair to begin to take the plates away. Alice said nervously but determinedly, "Tom, sit down please." Wyatt sat. "Why did you follow me?"

"To help," he said.

"You said," Alice replied. "Is there more?"

"And once I saw you and we began to talk," Wyatt gulped, trying to find the words, "something came over me. I wanted to help. No more than that ... felt compelled,

I'm not sure how to say it, to be with you; to help, not just practically but emotionally too; to ..., and this sounds corny and melodramatic, to save you."

"My knight in shining armour?" suggested Alice lightening the mood.

"If you can call clerical black shining armour," smiled Wyatt.

Alice returned the smile, "My saviour then."

"If you like," said Wyatt. "But you may not be the only one that needs saving."

Their eyes locked. Wyatt offered his hands across the table. Alice took them in hers and then they stood each taking the other in their arms, each one holding on as though to a lifebelt in a stormy sea.

Some moments later, they were sitting together on the settee sharing a bottle of wine.

Wyatt began, refreshed and invigorated. "While you were at work, I was thinking about Brett's contact list." Wyatt brought out the phone and pulled up the list. "Let me read them through: Anchor, Bitch, Cawdor, Chipper, Cow, Donkey, Fleur, Flipper, Grille, Heart, Imp, Judas, Kettle, Leech, Ozy, Palace, Pisa, Porker, Razor, Sniffer, Snooty and Winkle. Does anything resonate with you? People or places?"

Alice thought a moment. "We know about me and we've tried Anchor, Bitch and Ozy. Most seem random and mostly unflattering. Cawdor and Judas suggest traitors."

"I've heard of Judas," Wyatt smiled. "But Cawdor?"

"Shakespeare's *Macbeth*. Cawdor betrayed King Duncan. Could be just a place in Scotland though," Alice added.

"Anything else stand out?" asked Wyatt.

"Snooty. Lord Snooty. *Beano* character. Rich toff," suggested Alice.

"Or someone just stuck up," said Wyatt. "Donkey, Cow, Leech, Porker, Sniffer, Winkle. All animal connotations. All kind of derogatory."

"And some of the others suggest eating outlets," offered Alice. "Chipper, Grille, Kettle; maybe Palace, Pisa too."

"None of them sound like friends though," said Wyatt.

"True," replied Alice, "and no one has tried to contact him yet."

"Also true," said Wyatt. "How about we make just three more calls. If we draw a blank, we report him missing to the police."

"Okay," agreed Alice. "Any preferences?"

"Flipper sounds pretty innocuous. Let's try that," said Wyatt tapping the number. A moment later. "No answer. Just voicemail."

"Try Cawdor. Sounds nasty," suggested Alice.

Wyatt tapped. "Voicemail again. This is hopeless. Last one to you, Alice."

"Who knows? Grille?" Alice suggested half-heartedly.

The phone rang. "Laxton's Barbecue and Grille," came the reply. The voice was female. It sounded young.

Wyatt perked up. "Hello, I'm looking for a friend of mine. I wonder if you know him. Brett Barron."

"I'm sorry we're a restaurant," replied the girl. "We have lots of customers. I don't recognise the name. We're busy now. I'm sorry I can't help."

The phone went dead.

"At least we have the name of a place," said Wyatt.

"Yep and I've just googled it. It's a nice looking restaurant. In Bristol."

"That's a Bristol connection," said Wyatt. The Anchor and the Grille. There's got to be a link somewhere. We have at last something to go on."

"Maybe," Alice sounded doubtful. "Bristol's a big city."

"I fancy a day trip, and I've got nothing else to do," said Wyatt raising his glass. Alice mirrored him. They chinked and smiled together.

"Good luck, Tom. Here's to slim and tenuous."

"Sounds like names from Brett's contact list," said Wyatt.

They laughed together in an explosion of relief and moved in closer together.

28

The work was slow and painstaking. There would be hours of taking measurements and photographs, of taking notes and ticking checklists. Larry worked inside the galley while his colleague checked the ground outside, and the hedge and field beyond.

Larry emerged after half an hour and approached Kate. "There's plenty to do yet, Kate but here's something to be getting on with." Larry handed over a plastic ziplock which contained what looked like personal effects: wallet, phone and keys.

"Thanks, Sherlock. Looks like we know who he is."

"A John Graham. Driving licence will give you his address."

"Great, I'll get on to it," said Kate.

"Before you go, Kate, there's also this..." Larry brought his arm from around his back and held out another ziplock like a suitor presenting flowers to his young love. "Cocaine. Here about one hundred grams. More inside. You have a serious dealer on your hands. Just sign the chitty, Kate and I'll get back to the grindstone."

Kate signed the evidence form. "And I'll get back to the furnace."

The station was buzzing with expectation. Word had got round about a professional killing and a big drugs haul.

Sheldon was the first to greet her. "The boss wants to see you now ma'am." There was an edge of excitement in his voice.

Kate passed the ziplocks to him. "Thanks, Joe. Start finding out what you can about a John Graham."

"Ma'am." Sheldon took the plastic folders and turned to his computer.

Superintendent Fordyce was standing in front of his desk as Kate entered. He, too, appeared excited. He was shifting his weight from side to side like a barefoot bather on a hot promenade. He was also looking pleased. His voice squeaked with a suppressed delight.

"Inspector. Dreadful event, but a good opportunity to show what we're capable of. I know the big boys at regional HQ want to get their hands on this but I've made it clear we have the people and resources to get to the bottom of this. That's why I'm putting you in charge."

"Sir," Kate acknowledged. She glanced over his shoulder to see the photograph of Fordyce standing next to the local Member of Parliament, a man tipped to be a future prime minister.

"I know you've a lot on with the Goodwin stabbing...murder," Fordyce corrected, "and one or two other things, but I'll give you what you need within reason. Sergeant Sheldon looks ready to take on more. And if you get an early result, which I fully expect you will, then you will do this station proud. Keep me informed. That's all."

"Sir," said Kate in confirmation and left feeling

determined and undaunted. Perhaps it is in the nature of superintendents to be proud, she thought, but Fordyce's manner suggested the hubris of someone who was looking forward to the dubbing of a sword on the shoulder but might very well end up with a custard pie in the face.

Kate drew the attention of the office.

"We have two murders, two priorities. Both different but both important. We can handle them in parallel but not one at the expense of the other. A board each side of the office will collate key information. Sergeant Sheldon and I will focus on the John Graham murder. Sergeant Benson and Constable Turner, I want you to consider next steps in the Goodwin case. I suggest you go back over all the witness statements, contact them all and see if you get any video footage from their phones. Anything at all that might give a lead. I know that will be slow, laborious and unglamorous, but necessary. Follow any idea that comes to you, and Sergeant Benson," Kate said looking at him directly, "I know you've seen it all before, and you're looking forward to your retirement, but I'd like you to show our new Constable Turner the best, and not to tarnish her idealism and enthusiasm with your cynicism."

"Yes, ma'am," said Benson. "Does the mean that catnapping is off the agenda?"

"It does for now," smiled Kate.

29

Lee Thompson was tense. He wiped the perspiration from his palms on to his trousers. He ran his tongue over his dry lips. He waited for Levinson to begin.

"Coffee?" offered Levinson.

Thompson shook his head. He wanted this over with.

"Any last requests?" continued Levinson.

Thompson shook his head again.

"Don't be worried, Lee," said Levinson with a soothing menace. "Last requests that is before you start a new career."

Thompson shook his head again.

"No. Then let's look at the terms of future employment. First of all, I am delighted to tell you that your debts are cancelled. All of them. That was the reward for dealing with Ritchie Goodwin. You did it well. Cheer up. You should be proud of yourself."

Thomson shifted nervously in his chair.

"The police have nothing to go on. No CCTV. No witnesses. You're in the clear. You got rid of the knife, I take it."

Thompson nodded.

"Good. Then the only way this can go pear-shaped for you is if you give yourself away. If, however, you do get caught, let there be no misunderstanding. You will not mention my name – at all." Levinson stressed the final two words. "Is that clear?"

"Yes, Mr Levinson," replied Lee.

"You do realise you could go down for, let's say, about ten years, reduced to five with good behaviour," said Levinson.

Lee gulped. Beads of sweat began to form on his forehead.

"That may seem a long time, Lee, but look at it this way. The stretch is not much longer than some university courses, at the end of which you will no doubt have acquired many skills but you will also be a very rich young man."

Lee perked up with a look of questioning interest on his face.

"Because," continued Levinson, "there will be a lump sum of one million pounds to collect, a sum which I have set aside for you as a loyalty bonus."

Lee's eyes shone with future dreams.

"Not a bad result for someone who will still be in their twenties. Don't you agree?"

"Yes, Mr. Levinson," replied Lee, more encouraged.

"So, let us be perfectly clear, if the evidence against you is incontrovertible, accept it, plead guilty and thereafter stay silent. The reward for your silence and loyalty is wealth beyond your imagination." Levinson approached him and put an arm around his shoulder as an encouraging parent might. He leaned towards his ear and said, "Trust is so important in business."

Lee felt Levinson's breath in his ear and shuddered. He gripped the chair, unable to move, like a startled rodent before a venomous snake.

Levinson stood back, tapped him on the shoulder, returned to his desk and in a lighter advisory tone said, "Keep a level head; keep away from temptations and focus on your new career. I foresee a great future for you. Do you like the sound of that?"

Thompson nodded.

"You're very quiet, Lee." Levinson leaned towards him. "Say, I like the sound of that Mr. Levinson."

Thompson looked at the hard, cold eyes before him and uttered, "I like the sound of that, Mr. Levinson."

"Good," said Levinson, leaning back. "You must be wondering what your new job is. Let's put it this way. I think you would be an asset to the motor trade. In a day or two you will be offered the job of manager of Town and Country Motors. Do you like the sound of that?"

"Yes, Mr. Levinson." Thompson began to relax and exhaled in relief.

"It will be offered to you by George Stevens. You must know George. He's a friend of your father. It's a steady business, nice showroom, good workshop, pleasant staff. Your duties will involve maintaining the smooth running of the business. All legit, nothing dodgy. No favours, no special deals, no under the counter, no tax fiddles. Everything above board, traceable and accountable. Do you understand?"

"Yes, Mr. Levinson."

"And you think you can manage that?"

"Yes, Mr. Levinson."

"You will have to travel a little, collecting and delivering cars. On those journeys you will be also taking and receiving packages. You will be told where and when to go. You will ensure safe delivery and receipt. You will not ask questions. You will not open anything. For your, let us say, professionalism in this matter you will be well paid."

Thompson nodded again, a little more relaxed, as though a ray of sunlight had just pierced a turbulent sky.

"But be warned, Lee. Big pay brings big responsibilities, and if you are not up to it there will be big consequences." Levinson looked darkly and deeply into Thompson's eyes until Thompson looked down and wiped his palms once more on his trousers.

As Thompson walked away from The Black Cat, his stride grew more confident. The past was the past; the slate was wiped clean. As at the end of winter there was the hope of Spring ahead.

Levinson turned on the radio then went over to a shelf in the corner of his office on which there was a chess board set for a match in progress. He moved the white pawn forward.

"...and we interrupt this broadcast," the announcer said, "to bring you news that the body of a man has been found at a transport café at Cotedge layby. Police are appealing for witnesses..."

Levinson turned off the radio, smiled and moved the black knight forward to attack the opponent's rook. He took out his phone and deleted Geordie's details. It was then he noticed he'd had a missed call. He knew the name and number. He turned back to the chessboard and gazed in intense contemplation as he considered his next move.

30

"We have his address from his driver's licence and we know a bit about him. He's on file," said Sergeant Sheldon, "but not charged with anything."

"What was it?" said Kate.

"A complaint by his wife of assault. Later withdrawn," replied Sheldon. "Also he goes by the name of Geordie Graham. Ex-army. Logistics."

"Okay," said Kate. "Let's go and see her to break the sad news and on the way back we'll see if forensics have managed to get anything useful for us."

Sheldon weaved the car through the labyrinth of Summer Heights. He knew where to find Lamb Close. It was behind the play park towards the top of the hill that suggested the name of the estate to the first planners.

The play park had long given up its purpose. The witch's hat, a roundabout suspended from a central pole, listed into the mud, immobile. The frames for the swings dangled chains but no seats. What was once a rabbit on a fat spring now lacked ears and the handlebars coming from its cheeks. On what was left was sitting a youth, cigarette in mouth, arms outstretched, tilting to keep his balance, in a mockery of a Western rodeo. He might have impressed his companion, an adolescent girl but, at the very moment Kate and Joe drove by, his arms windmilled and he fell ignominiously to the bare earth. A dog nonchalantly passed, cocked its leg against the spring and trotted on.

Joe and Kate drew up to house. Cars were parked on the deeply rutted grass verges. The front garden was unkempt; paint was peeling from the front door.

"Yeah, what do you want?" a surly young male asked on opening the door. He looked to be in his late teens. He had a pale face with a few angry-looking spots. Wispy hair grew from his chin. His hair was tousled and he smelt.

Kate showed her ID. "Is Mrs. Graham in?"

"No," the youth replied. "She's gone. Left."

"May we come in?" asked Kate.

"S'pose," said the youth and turned.

Kate and Joe followed him into the sitting room. The first impression was of domestic chaos; the second was of helplessness.

The coffee table and easy chairs were festooned with takeaway boxes and foil trays; squashed beer cans and empty bottles vied for space; an ashtray was piled high with roach ends; there was the heavy scent of dope in the air. In the corner a television flickered in front of which sat, fixated, another youth deftly manipulating a handset.

"Hey, what you doin'," this one said as Sheldon pulled the plug from the socket in the wall.

"We need your attention," said Sheldon. "Both of you.

Make yourselves comfortable."

The youth by the television turned and faced inwards but remained seated on the floor; the one that had showed them in pushed a pizza box from an easy chair and sat down. Kate picked up from the settee a foil tray, yellow stained, put it on the coffee table, dusted over the seat with her hand and sat down. Sheldon remained standing, notebook in hand.

Kate addressed the one with the wispy chin. "You are...."

"Gordon," he said, "and he's Hamish. If you're looking for me mum, she's not here. If you're looking for me dad, he could be anywhere. He comes back when he feels like it."

"When did your mum leave?" Kate continued.

"A couple of days ago."

"Because..."

"She'd had enough of me dad, us, this place. Who knows?"

"And where might she go?"

Gordon shrugged.

"Any other family?"

"She's got a sister in London somewhere."

"How do you look after yourselves?"

"Dad gives us cash every so often. Enough to keep us going. We're okay. We're managing." Gordon sniffed.

"It's about your dad that we're here. I'm afraid to tell you that John Graham..."

"Geordie. Everyone calls him Geordie," interrupted Gordon.

"...that Geordie was found dead this morning, in his café. We suspect foul play."

"Shit happens," said Gordon, shrugging.

Hamish turned back to the television and pushed the plug back into the socket.

"We need to look around," continued Kate.

"Help yourselves," said Gordon. "We've got nothing to hide." He leant over to the table, took a joint out from under a pizza box, lit it, inhaled deeply and relaxed back into his chair.

Kate rolled her eyes at Joe and indicated with a slight movement of her head that they should leave the room and begin their search.

They started upstairs, each taking a separate room and went about their work quickly but methodically. Cupboards, drawers and shelves were efficiently checked. In some ways the sheer untidiness made their task easier. There was no hiding place for bulkier items like stashes of drugs, money or weapons. It was beginning to look like Geordie didn't bring his work home.

"See if you can find any paperwork," said Kate. "Anything at all that might have a name or address on it. Invoices, business cards, also phone or tablet."

"Yes, ma'am," replied Joe from the next room. "Nothing so far bar a pack of cards and a few porn mags."

"Keep your mind on the job, Joe. I'm not convinced that's evidence," replied Kate. "Nothing obvious in the bathroom either. Let's try downstairs."

Again their search was efficient and methodical. They left the sitting room till last. Gordon and Hamish looked as if they hadn't moved. Kate and Joe worked around them. So far nothing. Kate went over to a side table on which there was a photograph. It was a picture of Geordie with three of his army mates. They looked to be relaxing after an exercise. They were in fatigues standing in front of an open tent, each a beer in hand saluting the camera. One had a cigarette in his mouth.

"Do you mind if I take this? Kate asked Gordon.

Gordon glanced quickly. "No, not bothered. Up to you."

Kate removed the photograph from its frame and slipped it into her pocket.

"Gordon, I'm going to have to send a team round to do a thorough search. I suggest you tidy up a bit and get rid of the dope. Wouldn't want you getting into trouble."

Gordon shrugged. "Shit happens."

And despite the appalling situation, the years of neglect and emotional poverty, the sheer fecklessness that surrounded and infected the lives of those boys, Kate couldn't stop herself thinking in reply: And it usually comes from arseholes.

"First thoughts," said Kate to Joe as they were heading out of Summer Heights.

"The state those lads are in looks like twenty years of crime, but as regards the killing of Geordie. Nothing. Is it a drugs issue or something else? Who did he upset so badly to get himself shot? Who killed him? What does the wife know? Is her leaving significant?"

"As usual, Joe. more questions than answers. Let's see if the doc, Sherlock and the rest can give us something to go on."

31

It was a good job Wyatt was in no particular hurry that Tuesday morning. The tailback seemed huge, but at last he saw the blue flashing lights a few hundred metres ahead. Accident, he thought. Still, nearly past it. Clearly something serious had happened. A screen had been erected. As he passed by he crossed himself and muttered a prayer that would do for the injured or the dead.

After that the route was clear. A lovely sweep down the edge and onto the M5. Bristol in less than an hour. For a moment Wyatt was filled with the excitement and expectation of a day out on a new adventure. The refuel light pinged which made Wyatt think that not only did he need more petrol, but that he had better be careful. Perhaps Brett Barron was not just missing; perhaps he just didn't want to be found.

With the aid of Google and a satnav, The Anchor was easy enough to find. It was situated just off the Old Town between the hospitals and Queen Square in one of those narrow streets that have a nostalgic charm during the day and become flasher and brasher in the evenings.

Wyatt had to park some distance away and make his way on foot. The streets seemed busy enough with shoppers and office workers. There was a sense of purpose in the air as well as confidence that came with comfortable wealth. To Wyatt the women looked chic and the men looked smart. Suits and smart overcoats seemed the order of the day. Colourful scarves blended with silk ties in a kind of urban *feng shui*. Wyatt looked at his fleece and felt conspicuous.

It was just after noon. He walked past The Anchor and glanced. His view through the window was restricted by the name and image of an anchor frosted onto the glass, but he could see there were a few people in there: a couple at the bar and one or two seated together and separately at tables.

A sign outside listed the meals on offer. The fare looked simple and wholesome, the price immodest. In for a penny, thought Wyatt as he entered. The room was extensive but exuded a general sense of warmth and comfort. On the far side a log burner offered a welcoming glow. Solid, dark, wooden tables, some with burnished copper tops, were set against padded benches of deep reds and greens on the one side and complementary chairs or stools on the other. The walls were arrayed with mirrors and old photographs of the dockyards and its workers. The bar itself gleamed with a deep brown lustre, and the yellow lights in globe shades bounced their beams back and forth from mirrors to glassware to brass fittings. The place glowed warmly and snugly.

Wyatt sat at the bar and ordered a sparkling mineral water. The barman looked to be in his forties, clean-shaven, round-faced, slightly receding hairline. He wore a crisp white shirt, black waistcoat and black tie. He didn't say anything as he put down the drink on a thin paper drinks' mat which he seemed to conjure from thin air like a street magician.

ABSOLUTION

Wyatt nodded and wondered if that was the person he had spoken to on the phone. The barman moved off to see to another customer. He hadn't asked for money nor apparently had expected Wyatt to pay straight away.

Wyatt looked around. One or two more people came in, ordered drinks or meals and sat down. He thought he could tell first time customers by the way they looked around as he had done; regular customers were given drinks without asking. Sometimes there was a nod or a brief exchange but the overall mood was of a kind of reverence, a mutual respect, a politeness to observe one's privacy, an acceptance that one was not to be disturbed. Not dissimilar to a church, Wyatt thought.

Wyatt raised his hand. The barman came over. "I'd like to order a ploughman's please."

"Certainly, sir. Would that be the major or the minor?"

"I didn't realise there were different sorts. What's the difference?" queried Wyatt.

"Quantity and price." The barman cocked an eye.

"Minor please," replied Wyatt, not knowing whether he was being made fun of.

The barman retreated.

The bar began to fill but not uncomfortably so. Once or twice he noticed somebody, sometimes a man, sometimes a woman, would nod to the barman and continue through to the toilets, then return a few minutes later, nod again and leave. Wyatt's thought was of a lunchtime takeaway, a sandwich or even a minor ploughman's, packed carefully into a briefcase or shopping bag to be enjoyed back at the office.

"This looks lovely," said Wyatt as the barman placed the plate in front of him. The presentation of shapes and colours on the oval plate were enticing. Four kinds of cheese from pale cream to deep yellow were set against the bright green of fresh lettuce and the deep red of ripe sliced tomatoes; a thick slice of freshly made home-cooked ham guarded relishes of sweet chutney and piquant aubergine and was topped with sliced rings of red onion. The dish was accompanied by chunky slices of artisan sour dough bread and a pot of soft fresh butter.

"You should see the major," said the barman.

Seeing that as an opportunity to engage the barman, Wyatt said. "I'm pleased I dropped in. I was recommended to by a friend. Brett Barron. Perhaps you know him?"

The barman looked quizzical and pouted his lips. "Brett Barron? You say he's a friend of yours. A good friend?"

"The friend of a friend actually," replied Wyatt.

"And who would that be?" questioned the barman.

Wyatt was beginning to feel flustered. This wasn't supposed to be like this. The questioning was going the other way.

"To tell you the truth, he has your number on his contact list, so I thought you might know him. Why would he have your number otherwise?"

"Search me," replied the barman. "Perhaps he had a nice ploughman's here one day and thought he might come back."

Wyatt was unconvinced. "Is there anyone else here he would be in contact with? The manager maybe?"

The barman shook his head and turned away to serve another customer.

Wyatt finished his meal. He tried not to flinch when he saw the bill. On leaving he passed a note to the barman and said, "I'm trying to find Brett. If he shows up would you mind contacting me on this number."

"Can't promise, sir. We're not a lost property service," replied the barman and, as Wyatt turned away, he scrunched the note and dropped it into the bin.

Let's hope I have more luck at Laxton's Barbecue and Grille, thought Wyatt unconvinced as he walked back to his car.

32

"Sherlock," said Kate, "I hope you can give me more than we already know. We've just come from the pathologist and he told us no more than he did yesterday."

"That's not strictly true," said Sheldon. "He used more words and most of them were in Latin."

Larry Holmes laughed. "I promise not to use any Latin, but I can tell you some things and make educated guesses about others. Fact: he was killed with a bullet from a Russian P96 9mm semi-automatic. We found the shell lodged in a tree directly behind the bus."

"That's not a common weapon," said Kate, "so that suggests what? A hit? Organised crime?"

"Turf wars, maybe," suggested Sheldon.

"The quality of the shot suggests someone was either very lucky or a professional," said Larry.

"Professional, I'd say," said Kate. "A clean hit, no traces, no witnesses. Are these weapons traceable?"

"In my experience," said Larry, "virtually impossible."

"But why a Russian pistol?" asked Sheldon.

"My guess," said Kate, "would be a black market weapon. Any soldier that has been, for instance, to Afghanistan in the last ten years could have brought one back. Maybe just a trophy. The markets in Kabul have stalls full of Russian militaria. Some of it on show, most under the counter."

"How do you know this stuff?" asked Sheldon.

"My husband told me. Infantry captain, Two tours."

Sheldon nodded in respect. "Are we looking at a military connection then? Geordie Graham was in the army."

"Possible, but tenuous. Given the time he's been out and the quantity we recovered, a drugs connection might be a stronger line to pursue," said Kate.

"What about his wife?" suggested Sheldon. "It looks as though she wasn't happy. Would she be unhappy enough to have him killed?"

"Again, unlikely but we ought to try and find her Joe. We might get more background," said Kate.

"Can I suggest," interrupted Larry, "that you also check his phone? I know these guys are clever and find a million ways to cover their tracks, and you might never get past the security, but I do have at least one lead you can try."

"And that is, Sherlock?" said Kate.

"Bazzer."

"Bazzer!" exclaimed Kate.

"Yep, Bazzer. It's the last call he received. It came in

yesterday evening. No message. It was as though whoever it was was waiting for Geordie to speak."

"Okay, that might be something. We'll leave it with you, Sherlock. Let us know if you come up with anything."

"Audentes fortuna iuvat", said Larry to their retreating backs.

"What does that mean?" Sheldon asked Kate.

"No idea," said Kate. "Life's a lottery?"

"Maybe he's got an expensive dentist," suggested Sheldon.

They chuckled their way back to the car.

33

Johnny Thompson was at ease with himself. He enjoyed being a councillor and a mayor; he enjoyed his income; he enjoyed his friends, his comfort and his status. Most of this enjoyment derived from the fact that he didn't have to do any graft. There were no onerous tasks, no long hours, no sweating with anxiety over unpaid bills or where the next penny was coming from.

Thompson and Thompson Estate Agents was doing very nicely. George Stevens had seen the potential twenty five years earlier and had backed the smooth talking, sharp dressing Johnny Thompson. Stevens retained a sizeable share but remained a silent partner. For all practical purposes, the business was Thompsons.

His ability to convince both buyers and sellers that he was acting in their best interests made him successful. He considered himself to be in the relationship business, a matchmaker to whom clients would come to find the perfect home, for which services they would be very happy to part with a pretty hefty introduction fee.

As the domestic business grew he branched into commercial properties and rentals, and in time opened three other offices within a ten mile radius. More than four he thought would be hard work, less than four wouldn't generate enough income and that income was not just from property transactions but the associated commissions and fees from mortgages, insurances, legal services and property maintenance. It never ceased to amaze him how much money could be made from just one sale.

He kept a desk in each of his offices and would sit at each one for an hour every week checking the accounts, chivvying the staff and gladhanding customers. Other than that his time was his own to pursue his mayoral duties and his own pleasures.

If there was now a small cloud in the blueness of his sky, that would be his son Lee. Lee managed one of the offices but in recent months his behaviour had become erratic. The confidence and ebullience he had inherited from his father had drained and in its place was moodiness, ill-temper and lateness, not the best qualities for a people-centred business. Johnny had tried to speak to Lee about it but received a foul-mouthed tirade, the essence of which was that Lee did not like working in the family business, and he did not like living at home.

Johnny was disappointed but not surprised. The boy needed to be himself. He had been given everything, including the blanket that was beginning to smother him. It was time for him to be on his own.

Johnny's disappointment, however, gave way the following day to delight, if not elation when George Stevens phoned him to say he intended to offer Lee the managership of Town and Country Motors if he was interested. The position would be temporary in the first instance pending the return of the current manager.

The blue sky in Johnny's world was whole again.

34

Levinson was in his office. He had just finished speaking to George Stevens and was now making a round of calls to let those who needed to know that Barron was no longer on the scene and that his duties were being taken over by Lee Thompson who would introduce himself on the next occasion.

"That's good to know," said Phil Tyler, manager of The Anchor. "By the way, you should know that someone's just been in asking after Barron."

"Police?" queried Levinson, a note of alarm sounding in his voice.

"No, definitely not. I'm told this bloke is amateurish. He said he was looking for his friend. Thinks he's gone missing."

"Did he suspect anything?" asked Levinson.

"Jack the barman says not. Thought the bloke was naive, simple. Just looking for Barron, not for what he did."

"How did he get onto you?" queried Levinson.

"I think he's got hold of Barron's contact list. We had a call the other day. Seems now like it might have been the same bloke."

"Okay, Phil. Thanks." Levinson ended the call. He

thought for a moment then called Laxton's.

"Laxton's Barbecue and Grille," uttered a sweet female voice.

"Put Louis on now. Urgent. Tell him it's Levinson."

"Right away, Mr. Levinson."

A moment later. "Yes, Paul. Forget something?"

"Louis, there's a guy asking after Barron. Says he's a friend trying to find him. I think he may have Barron's phone. If he comes in I want the phone and I want him warned off. Not too heavy. Just enough."

"Got it," said Louis.

***

Wyatt had heard of the world-renowned suspension bridge but he had not realised how sumptuous and comfortable-looking Clifton itself was. The wide tree-lined streets gave proportion to the Georgian houses, some of which had been sub-divided into spacious apartments, but most of which looked to be whole. The sports cars and high-end SUV's which sat under the trees pointed to the wealth on which Clifton was built and still retained. From the right spot rich traders would have been able to see the tall-masted cutters and Guinea-men laden with tobacco and slaves and countless other cargoes making their way along the river towards the city docks and would have been calculating the profit before the ships had moored. No doubt rich traders still lived there alongside other high earners. Judges and lawyers, university professors, medical consultants, entrepreneurs and media creatives could enjoy each other's company and have all the advantages of a city with the exclusivity of a village.

Wyatt took a small gamble and parked in a residents' parking space about fifty yards from Laxton's Barbecue and Grille. A meal and limited small talk had elicited nothing at The Anchor. He didn't fancy another meal so this time he thought he'd be more direct and just ask the manager straight if he knew Brett Barron.

Having settled on his strategy he was just about to leave his car when he noticed a man and a woman, not together but one after the other, go into Laxton's. That's odd, he thought, I've seen them somewhere before. And then it came to him. They had walked past him at The Anchor, had gone through to the back and had returned a short time after. A few minutes later the two emerged and made their way in different directions. Not a takeaway, then, thought Wyatt as he made his way to the restaurant.

Inside, the restaurant looked like a cross between an English country house and an American diner. It had the clean lines and layout of a top end diner without the bling, and the comfort of an old country hotel without the fustiness. At the far end the chefs, white hatted and coated were on display, flicking their wrists and darting their eyes like skilled circus jugglers.

A smartly dressed young woman, white blouse, black skirt approached. "A table for one?" she enquired

"No, I'd like to speak to the manager, please," replied Wyatt.

A small, round-faced, middle-aged, bald-headed man appeared. "Yes, sir. How may I help?"

"I'm looking for a friend of mine, Brett Barron. He knows this place. I was wondering if you had any idea where he might be?"

The man looked at Wyatt. "I think I may be able to help, sir. Come this way."

For a moment, Wyatt was too stunned to move. He was expecting to draw another blank. The quest was seeming hopeless. But now something positive. As he followed the manager past the juggling chefs he felt elation and trepidation in equal measure.

They entered a lobby behind the kitchen which gave access to the toilets, fire exit and a door which led to what Wyatt assumed were offices or accommodation above.

"This way, please, sir," said the manager as he pushed open the rear door and entered the yard.

Wyatt followed and the moment he set foot outside he knew he was in trouble. His arm was violently grabbed and he was swung round, his back against an adjacent wall, another hand forcing his chin upwards. He was pinned by two men, one on each side. The one on his left balled his fist and rammed it into Wyatt's stomach. Wyatt doubled up, spluttered, gasped for air, and then the pain came, deep and dense. Tears formed in his eyes. Intense physical pain had only ever been theoretical to him, something that happened to other people in the Bible, films and books. He had had to imagine it before. Now that he felt it, he realised the failure of imagination. The second blow was a kick to the groin. He shuddered. First nausea, then the sharpness as of a dagger followed by the long, deep, dull ache as though his lower stomach was being wrenched from his body. The vomit came next.

The manager frisked Wyatt and drew out a phone and a wallet. "Is this Barron's phone?"

Wyatt could hardly focus but shook his head and hoarsely gasped, "Mine."

The manager dropped the phone, stamped on it heavily and ground it to pieces under his foot. "You'll need a replacement. And now, let's see who you are." He riffled through the wallet, drew out a driver's licence and read, "Fr. Thomas Wyatt, The Lodge, St. Jude's Catholic Church, Shelbury."

The manager raised an eye and with a wry smile said, "You're a long way from your parish Father. I suggest you go back to tend to your flock and leave us poor pilgrims to find our own way to the Celestial City."

He nodded to the two heavies who dragged Wyatt by the armpits down the yard to the side exit and dumped him ignominiously in the passage beyond.

It took a while for Wyatt to gather himself enough to make his way to his car. He snatched the parking ticket from the windscreen, dragged himself in, pressed his hands against his lower stomach, took a deep breath and wept. It didn't cross his mind to offer a prayer of deliverance.

35

The large white boards in the office were big on space and short on detail. Sergeant Benson looked at the photograph of Ritchie Goodwin attached top centre. Underneath was written: video and CCTV – none. He turned to Constable Turner. "Fiona, how far have you got with checking the phone footage?"

"I've checked ten so far, Sarge," she replied. "About another twenty to go. Nothing yet."

"I've asked for all images from CCTV in the area," Benson added, "but little to go on, though I've got a shot of a couple having a feel and a fumble outside Smith's which knocks *Gone with the Wind* into a cocked hat. Still we press on."

Turner smiled and returned to her desk.

Kate said, "Sergeant, just for background add The Black Cat, Paul Levinson, manager and George Stevens, owner. Ritchie's death could be a random killing but it was deliberate. There is no such thing as a motiveless murder."

Kate turned to her own board. Geordie's name and a blow up of the photograph she'd got from Geordie's house were placed top centre. From there lines branched out to sub-headings: Cindy, drugs (cocaine), murderer, contacts. Each sub-heading had further lines awaiting completion. Sheldon picked up a felt tip pen and wrote 'Professional' and 'P36' under 'murderer', then "Bazzer' under contacts.

Sheldon said, "Ma'am, we're assuming it's a professional hit. That means someone gave the order." He approached the board and wrote 'ordered by' under 'Professional'. "And anyway," he continued, "how do you arrange a hit?"

"Good question, but really quite simple. High risk and reward businesses like drug dealing have built-in insurances, but like any insurance you have to pay the premium. At the lowest level, for a few quid, some thug will turn up and batter a miscreant. At the top end, say high distribution, for serious misdemeanours, a call is made to an anonymous contact. Details of the target are provided. A fee is paid. Job done. When you're in the big league the number comes as part of the deal. The premium is included in the contract, as it were. Like a home owner you might never ever need to call on your policy, but when you need to you're pleased you've covered yourself."

"Are the calls and the money traceable?" asked Sheldon.

"The tech guys tell me they haven't traced any yet. It's all to do with electronics bouncing around the world, different servers on different continents."

"Can a hit be stopped?" asked Sheldon.

"Unlikely. Once the money has been received, job done."

"How much does it cost?"

"Negotiable. But about five grand would do it."

"Not much for a life," said Sheldon.

"A pocketful of coke," replied Kate.

Sheldon looked once more at the photograph on the board. "It's funny, ma'am, but I think I've seen that face somewhere. But for the life of me, I couldn't tell you where."

At that moment Superintendent Fordyce entered. "Progress, Inspector?"

"Not a lot yet, sir. No obvious leads from scenes of crime. Sergeant Sheldon is going to follow up on Cindy Graham, more for background and possible contacts. I'm going to check if his army past leads anywhere."

"Good work," he leaned in towards Kate. "If I could just have a private word, Inspector. In my office." Fordyce headed back to where he came from.

Kate turned to Sheldon, grimaced, then followed.

"Inspector. Kate, if I may be so bold," began Fordyce. I've an unusual request. I wonder if you would accompany me to dinner tomorrow evening."

Kate looked quizzical, taken aback.

"All above board," continued Fordyce, noticing her reaction. "For form's sake. You see, Mrs. Fordyce is not too well, nothing serious, but she's not up for the Highfield Shoot dinner. An annual occasion at George

Stevens' place."

Kate's interest was piqued.

"It's a semi-formal do following on from the day's shooting. Select group: Stevens, the mayor, myself, one or two others and their partners. Well what do you say?"

On any other occasion, Kate would politely but very firmly have told the Superintendent where he could stick the suppository of his invitation, but the opportunity to meet Stevens, maybe to get an insight into the man, his businesses, his relationships with Ritchie Goodwin and Levinson, proved too much of a temptation.

"I'd be delighted to sir," replied Kate.

"Norman, please," beamed Fordyce. "I'll pick you up just after seven." And with a hop and a skip he made his way to his chair.

Kate was already out of the door. She had to phone an old contact.

36

It had been Levinson's suggestion and it was not at all bad all things considered, mused George Stevens as he waited for Lee Thompson to settle himself in the chair opposite. He was smartly dressed and had a confident and competent air about him.

"Consider your being here not so much an interview as an introduction. I am aware of your experience in retail property sales with Thompson and Thompson, and though your father will miss you, he feels that a move would suit you well. Is that right?" said Stevens.

"Yes, Mr. Stevens. I'm ready for a fresh challenge and more responsibility."

"You know, of course, that what I'm offering is temporary pending the return of the current manager, whose absence I must say remains a mystery but, if you prove yourself to be as successful as you promise to be, then I'm sure there would be other opportunities available in my organisation."

"Thank you Mr. Stevens. I'll repay your trust and confidence," returned Lee.

Stevens stood up. Thompson followed. They shook hands.

"Welcome to Town and Country Motors. I should add that I'm not an interfering owner but the absence of Brett

Barron as well as other things has made me think I need to keep a closer personal eye on what's happening. I'll give you a few days to settle in, to get to know the staff, get to grips with the finances and general running of the business. I'll let Sharon the secretary know. She'll be a great help to you. Expect to see me soon."

As Lee left, Stevens sat down. The boy seems good enough, he thought, not as sharp as Ritchie Goodwin maybe, but he looks as though he can sell cars and manage people. Also it's within the family, as it were, and that can only be good.

To someone who didn't have one, a family was very important indeed.

***

Lee drove steadily down the long drive of Highfield. He was relaxed. The job's a doddle, he thought, with a highly lucrative sideline. The owner's a gullible fool. Life's a breeze. As he met the lane beyond the gate, he put his foot hard down on the accelerator and sped off to the distant rise.

37

"Joe, any luck with tracing Cindy Graham?" asked Kate.

"No, still trying", said Sheldon. "The guys at the Met are not hopeful. Not enough to go on."

"Okay. See what you can make of Bazzer. Anything on file?" A long shot I know. I'm going to see if the army can help."

"Ma'am," replied Sheldon.

By 'army' Kate meant the unofficial route. Her experience of official channels was that they were long, ponderous, obstructive and ultimately unproductive.

"Kate," said Mark Hornton, answering his phone. "How lovely to hear from you. All well?"

"Fine, Mark. All good in the hedge fund business?"

"Can't complain. Just a shade off three hundred grand last year. Not bad for having a keen eye and a quick finger."

"I guess it beats being a major in the army," said Kate, "and it's the army I'm phoning up about." She thought she heard an intake of breath and a hesitancy.

"And how can I help?" said Hornton.

"I have a photograph of some guys. Looks as if they're

on tour or exercise somewhere. I'm not expecting you to know them but maybe you could help identify their units or regiments from any insignia and, if I'm lucky, where the photograph was taken."

"Shouldn't be a problem," said Hornton. "Send it now."

Kate took and sent the picture. It was received almost instantaneously. "The guy second from the left is John Graham. Goes by the name of Geordie. He was murdered yesterday in what looks like a professional hit. What do you think?"

"Honestly, Kate," came the reply. "I don't think I can be any help at all. Got to go. Lovely to talk." The phone went dead.

Kate sat back. Her emotional memory clicked. She had had the same feeling years before when she had tried to find out from him about Martin's death. She was convinced Hornton knew something but he was unwilling, unable or too frightened to tell.

38

Alice could tell from Wyatt's face and demeanour that he had not had a good day. He began to tell her what happened but the telling gave way to the pain and, as he looked at her, tears started in his eyes. He looked down in embarrassment and muttered in a tone more objective than self-pitying, "Some knight."

She came to him and touched his face, and all at once that tender action turned into a frenzy of feeling and fumbling, of peeling and mumbling, of tugging and tearing, of kissing and groaning, of touching and tasting, of pulling and squeezing, of fondling and moaning. And as they spent themselves Alice's spirit soared in blissfulness and Wyatt's grace crashed in ecstasy.

39

The sun was strengthening, giving hope that winter was behind and that warmer times were ahead. The pheasant season was coming to an end and the day looked set perfect for a comfortable bag.

The Highfield Shoot was a select affair. It could have been a business but George Stevens had enough businesses. For him his pheasant shoot was a hobby, a pastime he could share with his friends. Today he had invited Johnny Thompson, Norman Fordyce and Jim Curtis, his ever obliging bank manager. As he stood in the barnyard two hundred metres behind Highfield he awaited his guests. Beside him stood Len Fox, his keeper.

"Looks a good day for it, Len."

"Very good, Mr. Stevens," returned Len. "The birds are well situated. There should be plenty to shoot at."

"Enough beaters?" asked Stevens.

"Yes, the usual crew," replied Len. "All prepped. All know what to do. As usual, Billy's on the game cart and Mick and his missus are picking up."

Stevens had not really any need to ask. Len Fox was as solid and dependable as an ancient oak. He was dressed in country tweeds and, but for his accent, weather-beaten face and worn hands, looked every inch the country squire. His keen eye and his light but stealthy gait, however, marked him out as a man of the land and woods.

A black Discovery pulled into the yard. At the wheel was Johnny Thompson.

"Great day for it, George," said Thompson, holding out his hand.

"Aim high and true," replied Stevens. "And here are the others," he said, raising his hand in greeting to a green Land Rover, out of which appeared Jim Curtis and Norman Fordyce.

"Hail fellows, well met," chirruped Curtis, followed by handshakes and greetings all round.

"Before we make the draw for the pegs," Stevens said, "Len will explain the format of the day."

Len cleared his throat. "Welcome, gentlemen. Firstly and most importantly, a safety announcement. I know you've all shot before but please remember to carry your gun safely between drives, and when you're ready to shoot, make sure there is clear sky behind the bird. We don't want any beaters losing eyebrows." Johnny Thompson shifted his weight and looked at the ground. "We'll be doing five drives," Len continued, "starting with Cornfield Rise. I'll set off now with the beaters. Mr. Stevens will escort you to the pegs when you're ready."

Len turned away and headed over to a covered trailer in which the beaters sat.

Stevens led the guns to the barn to make the draw. The pegs were decided by drawing numbered used shell cases from an old leather pouch. In reality, the draw was a customary formality for there was very little advantage to be gained from the particular position of a peg. What was most important was whether the birds flew over and the gun could gauge the position and height of the target, variables no keeper could guarantee.

"Let's use my Discovery," offered Thompson. "Plenty of room for guns, drinks and snacks." The others nodded, knowing that was probably going to be his only positive contribution to the day.

For the first drive, the pegs were situated in a depression behind field hedging. Thompson had to drive by lane and track about half a mile from the barn before he could park up. The guns had to walk the last quarter mile beside a stream in a low valley before they were in position.

Thompson was beside Stevens and said in a low voice so as not to let the others hear, "Thanks for taking on Lee. He was in need of a new challenge."

"He was recommended to me by someone who's a shrewd judge of people. You do know the post is temporary at the moment?" said Stevens.

"Yes but Lee said that if he proved himself you may have other opportunities."

"That's true. And as we're on the subject, let me say now, Johnny, that given the tragic loss of Ritchie Goodwin and the current absence of Brett Barron, I have decided to take a much closer interest in all of the businesses, including Thompson and Thompson. I think Ritchie was on to something somewhere. I want to know what it was."

"Great! I'll look forward to having you around. Nothing to hide. All ship shape and Bristol fashion, as they say," replied Thompson, not wholly convincingly.

"Good. And now for a good day's sport," said Stevens. "Here's your peg, Johnny. Remember: aim high!"

The guns settled themselves at their pegs and awaited the first flush. Len Fox controlled the operation, directing beaters through walkie-talkies to move steadily, to stop, to flag as necessary. At this time of the season some of the wilier partridges knew how to break out and fly well away from the guns, but the pheasants were more herdable and amenable and, with his sure knowledge and judgement Fox was able to create a steady series of flushes for the guns to enjoy. Fortunately for the birds most flew over the less experienced guns to find shelter in the woods behind. The unluckiest were those that flew into Stevens' range. After twenty five minutes Len blew his whistle to tell the guns the drive was over. The guns picked up their spent cartridges, left the downed birds for the pickers-up and their dogs to retrieve, and made their way back to the Discovery to head off to the next drive.

"How was that?" Stevens said to Fordyce.

"Terrific," said Fordyce. "I got one or two. Plump cocks, too."

"I noticed you had plenty of shots," said Curtis, chipping in.

"Getting my eye in. What's the next drive, George?" asked Fordyce.

"Lacewing Wood," said Stevens.

"My favourite," said Fordyce, as the three headed off chatting to the Discovery.

Johnny Thompson was a few yards behind, counting in his pocket his spent cartridges. Fourteen shots and not one hit to account for. Things were not going well and that was beginning to trouble him.

***

After Lacewing the guns took a break and availed themselves of a shot of whisky and some still-warm sausages which Stevens had arranged for his kitchen to prepare.

"Any progress yet, Norman, with you know what?"

"Early days, George, but I've got my best people on it, led by Inspector Kate Brown."

"That's the one that came to see my wife, isn't it? said Thompson. "She's very good, I'm told."

"Yes, she's one of the best," returned Fordyce. "In fact you'll all get to meet her this evening at dinner because she's coming as my escort. Unfortunately, my good lady is not feeling well and, for form's sake, I invited Inspector Brown. Hope that's okay with you, George?"

"By all means," said Stevens.

At that moment, a ray of sun broke out from behind a cloud and the whisky glinted a deep gold like burnished bullion. Stevens finished his tot and, feeling much fortified, said, "Well, gentlemen, now for Highfield Cover."

***

Three long blows on the keeper's whistle signalled the end of the day's shooting. The sky was darkening, the temperature dropping. A night frost was likely. The four guns looked around to each other and nodded in satisfaction.

"Great day, George," said Thompson. "I managed a few more than last time."

"And all beaters accounted for," quipped Fordyce.

The others chuckled.

As they made their way across the field in which the rape was pushing through the soil, Stevens held back with Curtis.

"Jim," Stevens began, "I'm going to take a greater interest in my affairs. I intend to conduct a close examination of the books over the last few years. I don't really expect to find anything untoward. The auditors would have alerted me, I'm sure. But it's not just my accounts I'm interested in. I want to know if there's anything unusual about those that work in or manage my companies, including..." Stevens nodded at Thompson's back.

"George, I can't do that!" expostulated Curtis. "Client confidentiality."

"Jim," emphasised Stevens, "I don't need to remind you that you have done very well out of the business I have put your way. One of the reasons, the principal reason I should add, why you are so highly thought of at Local Head Office. I'm sure you would like that to continue."

"Yes, but…" Curtis was struggling to calculate the risk benefit equation.

Stevens continued, "I don't need to know everything. Just what strikes you as unusual: money transfers, ghost companies, asset holdings, other directorships. Anything to suggest my employees are doing more than their day job. Shouldn't be too onerous. And, of course, it will remain completely confidential between us." Stevens stressed the word 'confidential'.

Curtis looked round. He saw the darkening wood and smelled the air, filling with sharp freshness and a pungency from the red-brown earth. He felt like a driven pheasant about to fly.

"Well, Jim."

"Yes, alright, George. But completely confidential."

"Completely," affirmed Stevens.

Curtis felt he had taken off and had no idea whether he would reach the safety and security of the woods beyond.

40

Kate looked at the photograph. Hornton's evasiveness had created an uneasiness in her which caused her to think that there was not only the past in play, but that there was a link to the present. Was that link to her, to Graham, or to something or someone else? It could be a wasted journey but what alternative did she have? It was her last chance at an unofficial route.

She turned to Sheldon, "If you find yourself at a loose end, see what you can find out about drug distribution in the south west. I'll be out for the day. Army business. See you later."

"Ma'am," replied Sheldon.

***

The drive east was pleasantly uneventful. The village of Lower Uppington was on the barely defined eastern edge where the light sandstone gave way to ironstone. There was no Upper or Higher Uppington though presumably there once was. The village had grown slowly over time, and though now small estates were taking root on the north eastern edge, the village retained a sense of stability and timelessness. The older buildings were constructed of ironstone under thatched or slated roofs, and in summer the stone would seem to glow like warm honey.

'The Close' was approached by a short but wide gravel drive from a small narrow street behind the church at the village centre. The proximity to the church suggested 'The Close', the land if not the building, had been linked to it in some way in the past. Other buildings, too, had established themselves over the centuries. The stone-built, slate-roofed, mid-nineteenth century church school was now a small library; the eighteenth century weavers' cottages were now an artisan pottery. What were once stables had been converted into one fine residence. Disparate as these buildings were in age and style, size and shape they seemed now to Kate as she came to a halt on the gravel to offer a world of tranquillity, comfortable wealth and social harmony with aspirations and values as solid and permanent as the buildings themselves.

Retired Lieutenant Colonel Francis ffrench-Fitzgibbon, late of the 1st Green Jackets greeted her warmly at the door and led her through to the sitting room where Mrs. ffrench-Fitzgibbon was also delighted to see her. He was of medium height with a round face of ruddy complexion. He had a broad smile which showed white even teeth, a perfect match for his trim hair. He had the look of a kindly grandfather. His wife was short, round, comfortable and discreet.

Aware that the visit was not principally a social one, Mrs. ffrench-Fitzgibbon politely withdrew and left the two together.

"Frank, I'd like your help. I sent a copy of this to Major Hornton," said Kate, handing over the photograph of Geordie Graham and his pals, "and the response was a blank. Not a denial, more like an evasion. Just like when Martin died. So I've come to you. You know Horton. You were Martin's mentor. You may know the significance of this picture. The one smiling with the can in hand raised highest is Geordie Graham, shot dead recently in what we believe to be a professional assassination. Do you know what it is?"

Retired Lt. Col. Francis ffrench-Fitzgibbon looked hard at the photo. His face darkened, his lips tightened. He cleared his throat. He handed the photograph back and said, "I know exactly what it is. That, my dear, is a can of worms."

"Meaning?" said Kate quizzically.

"Meaning," replied ffrench-Fitzgibbon, taking a deep breath, "that what I am about to tell you is shrouded in caveats, will raise ghosts, may not be proven, will almost certainly be denied and," he hesitated, "will cause you pain."

Kate looked at the retired Lieutenant Colonel then at the photograph and made the connection.

"You're talking about Martin, aren't you?" she said.

"Yes, I'm afraid so," said ffrench-Fitzgibbon.

Kate braced herself. "You'd better begin, Frank. I'm ready. I don't think you can hurt me more."

"They say the truth will hurt, Kate, but what I have to say is a mixture of facts, suppositions and guesswork. Most of the evidence for what I have to say is circumstantial. There may be others who know more but you're very unlikely to find out what they know."

"I know, Frank. I had the feeling I was being stonewalled years ago, that I was not being told the truth. But I'm curious, Frank," she continued, "why are you telling me now?"

"Well, for a start you never asked me and, even if you had done, I might have come across as obstructive as the others. Neither of us would have wanted that. I could speculate but mostly I was embarrassed by my own ignorance. A half-truth would have been more, not less, devastating than nothing."

"And why are you prepared to tell me now," said Kate.

"Simply time, distance and perspective. There are enough pieces of a shattered pot stuck together to suggest the whole."

"Are you not still bound by the Official Secrets Act?" queried Kate.

"Indeed I am, but I'm not giving away any official secrets, any more than that photograph is. What I have to tell you may help you with your investigation into Geordie Graham's assassination, and may help you understand, if not come to terms with the circumstances of Martin's death."

"I'm listening," said Kate, taking out her notebook.

"Of the four people in that picture only one, as far as I know, is still alive. Graham, as you know, is dead. The two at each end, Privates Rowlinson and Williamson, were killed together in a road accident some years ago. The one to the left of Graham is ex-Corporal Jock McAndrew, a capable soldier, a natural leader, tough and, when he needed to be, ruthless.

Whatever it was that attracted them to each other, maybe their backgrounds, maybe their aspirations, they did share a common trait: they were opportunists. And in Afghanistan, as in any conflict, there were plenty of opportunities for enterprising, organised risk-takers to make good money out of trading, they preferred to call it liberating, such things as food supplies, vehicle parts, clothing, even small arms and ammunition. Graham would certainly have known about the movement of stores from his previous experience with the Loggies."

"But if you knew this," said Kate, "Surely you could stop it."

"Easier said than done, Kate. You're looking at a conspiracy writ large, or rather a series of well-organised, interlinked networks of bright, motivated individuals. Also conflict brings confusion. Items get lost, destroyed; records are adjusted or just disappear. It's a natural and inevitable consequence of warfare. As leaders and managers we have to trust our subordinates and accept a certain amount of tolerance."

"So, theft is what these people were involved in," said Kate tapping the photograph in her hand. "And how was Martin involved?" Her voice trembled a little in anticipation of hearing something uncomfortable.

"Not theft," continued the Lieutenant Colonel, "at least if it started off as theft it developed beyond that. And this is where it becomes more speculative. These guys,

Martin suspected, were into something much more risky and potentially much more rewarding. They were into drugs: heroin to be more precise."

"And still are, or were. There's a good chance Geordie Graham's assassination is drugs related, but now it's cocaine," said Kate.

ffrench-Fitzgibbon nodded in confirmation. "We had heard of some consignments of heroin making their way back to the UK in equipment, and one or two soldiers had been caught in possession of relatively small amounts. We were getting a picture and it was pointing to McAndrew and his crew amongst others. I was tasked with finding out what I could, but had to go softly, softly. It was all suspicion, nothing really to go on, and the Ministry was anxious that nothing should get out into the press. You could imagine the field day the press would have had if it had found out the British Army was sustaining the Taliban by smuggling heroin into the UK."

"Embarrassing, to say the least," said Kate.

"Much more than that, Kate. Political reputations were at risk. The Defence Secretary was tipped to be the next PM."

"So you delegated Martin to investigate?" asked Kate.

"Martin was the closest officer to these men. He was their leader. He had their respect in military matters. He was utterly trustworthy. He was clever, cautious and alert. He would keep his eyes open. He knew the risks. He would report to me if he had anything concrete."

"So he never came up with anything?" asked Kate.

"Nothing substantial. He mentioned that his interpreter had got something he was following up. He gave me names including the ones on that photograph, but he died before we could get any further. There was just no proof."

There was a long pause. Retired Lieutenant Colonel ffrench-Fitzgibbon took a deep breath and continued, "As you know, Martin was an outstanding leader, a brave and courageous man. He died defending his men and his position."

Kate had heard this before. It recalled the letters of condolence from years before, but the Lieutenant Colonel's tone was beginning to fill her with dread. "But..." she said.

The Lieutenant Colonel continued, "Attacks and skirmishes are seldom clear affairs. There is close contact and often confusion. Accidents can happen."

"Accidents?" stuttered Kate.

"Martin wasn't killed by a Taliban bullet. The bullets that killed both him and his interpreter came from a British Army standard issue L85 assault rifle."

It took a moment for the significance to sink in.

"So he was killed by his own men."

"Yes, one or more."

"An accident?"

Lieutenant Colonel ffrench-Fitzgibbon shrugged his shoulders. "That's the official line."

Kate was still trying to absorb the information. "But I wasn't told. That's what hurts. You know what I think?" she continued.

The Lieutenant Colonel nodded, "Yes, I think I do."

"I think that all the evasion from Major Hornton and the others is because you really think that it wasn't an accident. That the attack on the base was used as an excuse to cover up a murder, a double murder, in fact. That an officer, my husband, my Martin was killed because he was on to something. The real enemy was on the inside and the authorities couldn't bear for the truth to come out."

"That's what I believe," said the Lieutenant Colonel, " but as I say, it's only supposition."

"You must have more than that, Frank. There was after all an attack on the base," said Kate.

"Circumstances suggest that maybe it was not an attack at all, but a delivery that went drastically wrong. You see, it's not usual to find a few bags of heroin on the ground and the pockets of a dead insurgent stuffed with dollars."

Kate nodded. "Thank you, Frank. You said the truth might hurt. But it doesn't. Martin died because he was a good man. I already knew that." Kate's voice was steady. She was not angry or shocked, but she was determined. "You know what this means, though," she continued.

"What would that be?" replied the Lieutenant Colonel.

"That my investigation into the death of Geordie Graham is now personal, and that this can of worms," she said waving the photograph before her, " has a bit more wriggling to do."

41

Levinson was in his office checking the balance sheets. The accounts were looking healthy. Converting the cash into property through a network of companies was surprisingly easy. And converting older houses into student lets washed the cash so thoroughly it was as clean and pure as a nun's wimple. It wouldn't be long, he thought, before he would be a completely legitimate businessman, but it would have been sooner if Geordie Graham hadn't tried to cut in and undermine his trade. Still, everything was back on track and looking rosy. He allowed himself to relax back in his chair and sip his coffee. Except, he frowned, for a little niggle, not necessarily threatening but an aggravating nuisance, all the same.

At that moment the phone rang.

"Yes, Louis."

"Paul, I thought you'd like to know about the guy who was showing an interest."

Levinson perked up and leant forward. "Yes, Louis, go on."

"You were right. He came asking about Barron but left none the wiser."

"He must have been disappointed," smiled Levinson.

"Deflated more like," quipped Louis. "He was short of

wind when he left."

"Who was he?" asked Levinson.

"You'll never guess. You could say he was looking for a lost soul," said Louis.

"You'll have to tell me. I'm no good at guessing games," said Levinson.

"You might know him. In fact you may be in his parish, if not in his flock. His name's Wyatt. Father Thomas Wyatt, parish priest of St. Jude's," said Louis.

"What! I don't get it," said Levinson, momentarily stunned. "I don't know him but I know where the church is. What is a priest doing looking for Barron?"

"As I said, lost soul," said Louis. "The Catholic Church has had a bad press recently. Can't afford to lose any worshippers. They need to keep all they can, even the dodgy ones."

"Did you get Barron's phone from him?" Levinson asked urgently.

"No, he didn't have it on him. And his own phone met with an accident," said Louis.

"Do you think he's likely to report to the police?" asked Levinson.

"Not a chance. I got the strong impression that he left us not just with a creased stomach and bruised balls, but with a huge dent in his pride. I don't really think he could explain to anyone, let alone the police, what he was doing in Bristol in the middle of January."

"Thanks, Louis. Good job," said Levinson.

"By the way, Paul, what has happened to Barron?" asked Louis.

Levinson replied, "He's moved on. Greener pastures and all that. Keep an eye on the new lad for me. Keep him straight." Levinson ended the call.

Levinson refreshed his coffee and pondered. The priest is looking for a missing person. He thinks Barron is alive, contacted probably by Barron's girlfriend who must be wondering where he is. Levinson smiled at the confusion his removal of the body was causing. If the priest hasn't got Barron's phone then the chances are it's at the flat. That should be easy enough to liberate, he thought. He could feel the little niggle beginning to fade.

He strode across the chessboard and studied it intently. Looks like mate in three, he said to himself, pushing his pawn forward to tempt the knight.

42

"Mummy, you look gorgeous," said Misha, as Kate walked into the sitting room. Her hair was down and the make-up was subtle and stylish. The deep green silk dress hugged her figure. Short pendant gold earrings caught the light and winked. Kate bent her head down to Misha.

"Just a peck, otherwise I'm going to have to start all over again," said Kate smiling.

"You do look a picture," said Granny. "I'd nearly forgotten how lovely you can look. I see you too often dressed for work. I hope you enjoy your date."

"It's not a date, Mum," said Kate. "It's work. And Superintendent Fordyce is not my beau. He's my boss. I'm saving him from social embarrassment. I only agreed to go because I'm interested in meeting a few of his friends for professional reasons."

"Who might they be?" asked Granny.

"The mayor, for one," said Kate.

Misha and Granny looked at each other and, in a mirroring action, raised their eyes, pursed their lips and nodded.

Kate smiled, "I knew you would be impressed. I don't spend all my time with criminals." Though as she said it she wasn't convinced it was entirely true.

The doorbell rang.

"That'll be the boss. I'll be off. I won't be late," said Kate closing the door behind her.

"Have a lovely evening," said Granny and Misha together, looking at each other and repeating the same facial expression.

Superintendent Norman Fordyce was beaming. He was dressed in a dinner jacket and sported a large bowtie with a pattern of pheasants on a green background. To Kate it looked faintly ridiculous and, aware that Kate was looking at it, Fordyce tugged it and said, "For the occasion," and then, "You look wonderful."

Kate accepted the compliment, "Sir."

"Norman. Please call me Norman," he said holding open the passenger door.

"Norman," she muttered, as she sat down, and hoped that the evening was not going to continue to be awkward and embarrassing.

Small talk was hard to come by so it was with some relief when they reached the gates of Highfield.

"A magnificent place," said Fordyce.

"It is impressive," said Kate with admiration. "George Stevens is a good friend of yours, sir...Norman?"

"We've known each other a long time. He's a good

man. He does a lot for charity. Works hard. Not bad at golf. Lost his wife a long time ago now. Never remarried."

"You said the mayor would be there. Anyone else?" asked Kate.

"Jim Curtis and his wife. Bank manager. Solid, dependable chap. Useful to know for car loans, mortgages and the like." Fordyce tapped the side of his nose and, in that single action, Kate understood more about Fordyce than she had gleaned in the last three years.

The car came to a halt with a crunch of gravel. George Stevens was there to welcome his guests. He opened the passenger door. "Delighted to meet you...", offering his hand and leading her gently out.

"Kate," replied Kate.

"Kate. Welcome. I'm George. Norman will show you in. He knows the way around." He turned to Fordyce, "The Thompsons are already here. I'll join you as soon as the last guests arrive." He nodded courteously as Kate and Fordyce walked past him and made their way up the flight of steps.

Leaving their coats with a maid in the hall, Fordyce showed her into an oak-panelled drawing room. From the high ceilings with its ornamental plasterwork hung two grand chandeliers in antique glass. Around the walls were hung a series of eighteenth century landscapes, now dulled with age. In the far corner stood a mini grand piano on which there was a photograph of a younger George Stevens with, what Kate presumed was, his wife. In the centre of the room standing close to a round mahogany table were three people. Kate knew one of them, guessed the other and had no idea who was the third.

The one she knew was Mrs. Thompson. She had dressed for the occasion, but to Kate looked like someone who had tried to impress but lacked the taste and the class. There was a jarring of colours and her jewellery was too gaudy to be anything other than street market bling. She also looked tense and uncomfortable like an overstretched elastic band. Beside her was her husband, the mayor, Johnny Thompson. It wasn't hard to guess. He, too, liked to impress for, though not a civic occasion, he wore his chain of office. In the circumstances it looked rather sad to Kate. Not only was it inappropriate but having the civic insignia hanging under that chubby, smug face somehow degraded rather than raised his status. The third person was the embodiment of graceful elegance. She was tall and slim. She wore a full length black evening dress. Her dark brown hair was pinned back and looked stylishly careless. Small cut diamond earrings matched the necklace around the delicate white of her throat. She held her cocktail glass like a precious flower. When she smiled the light caught the brilliance of her teeth and when she spoke her voice was reminiscent of the gentle fall of water rippling over pebbles in a summer brook. As regards age, Kate thought she could be anywhere in that broad indetermination between the early thirties and late forties.

Fordyce strode ahead. "Let me introduce my colleague, Kate Brown."

Everyone nodded in welcome.

"Kate, you've met Mrs. Thompson, I believe."

They smiled at each other.

"Call me Elaine," Mrs. Thompson said.

"This is Mr. Thompson or should I say Mayor Thompson," continued Fordyce.

"Johnny, please," said Thompson.

"And this delightful lady," said Fordyce, "is Florence Chambers, a friend of George."

"I'm pleased to meet you, Kate," said Florence.

As Fordyce turned to get some drinks, Thompson began for Florence's benefit, "Inspector Kate here has been helping us with a certain matter, hasn't she Elaine?" Mrs. Thompson nodded. "You see, we believe our cat has been kidnapped. Have you got anywhere with it yet?"

"No, I'm afraid not," said Kate, fearing her face betrayed her thoughts. She felt like a teacher invited to a party full of parents whose children she taught; or a doctor trying to have a drink in a pub full of patients; those that thought as a public servant you were there at all times to serve their selfish neediness.

Florence must have read her thoughts. Highfield is a wonderful house, Kate. If we have time, I must show you round after dinner."

"Thank you," Kate smiled, relieved, though she had to remind herself that she had chosen to be there on business and that some discomfort was to be the likely price of reward.

At that moment, Stevens entered with the Curtises and the dinner party was complete.

The centre piece of the dinner itself was a brace of beautifully roasted pheasants. There was some banter amongst the men, mainly at the expense of Thompson about how little shot was evident in the breast. The women indulged them condescendingly by smiling or rolling their eyes at each other, but for the most part they kept the conversation amongst themselves.

The staff were attentive. There was no sense of rush, and glasses were promptly filled. Dishes were cleared inconspicuously. Kate noticed that Stevens drank little whilst the other men overindulged.

When the last plates had gone and the port was offered, Thompson took it upon himself to propose a toast. He swayed as he stood. His face looked rounder and redder. Toasts were proposed to the ladies; to George; to the noble pheasant and to the Queen, after which Thompson sat down heavily and belched. The elastic band that was Mrs. Thompson stretched to whiteness.

"The drawing room for coffee," said Stevens.

"We'll join you soon, George," said Florence. "I promised Kate a quick tour of Highfield. We won't be long."

"Of course," said Stevens.

As the table disbanded and Kate and Florence made their way into the hall, Kate turned to Florence, "Thank you. I needed a break."

"I could see that. Sometimes these parties can be a trial. George feels obliged."

Kate nodded. "Yes. They don't seem a natural group of friends."

"Very astute. They're not really close. More like a mutual dependency, a self-help club," said Florence, then continued. "The house is Georgian with many period features, but I hope you don't mind if I don't point them all out. As we walk around, I'd rather talk about George, or rather what's worrying him. And I rather suspect you would find that more interesting."

"That's very astute of you, too," said Kate. They smiled at each other. For the first time that evening things were beginning to interest her.

"George is a self-made, self-reliant man. He believes his instincts about people and projects are sound, but recent events have unsettled him," said Florence.

"You mean the death of Ritchie Goodwin?" replied Kate.

"That certainly. He treated Ritchie almost as a son. He's thinking his death might not be random but connected in some way to his businesses. He intimated that Ritchie was about to tell him something, and was silenced before he could." Kate nodded. "And then there is the disappearance of the manager of his garage business."

Kate nodded again. "Yes, that was mentioned to me. Are you saying they're related?"

"George is beginning to think so," said Florence.

"If you don't mind me asking, Florence, why are you telling me this and not George?"

"George is a proud and private man. He takes these things personally. He sees them rather as a family matter, and as patriarch, as it were, he will want to sort things out for himself."

"Without involving the police?" asked Kate.

"He will use the police as he sees fit. You've seen how he is, indeed how they all are, with Norman. They all use each other. But he will seek justice for himself."

"I see," said Kate, feeling that she was in some kind of competition with an avenging angel and that she and the others had better find some answers before an otherwise seemingly good man fell from grace.

***

Farewells followed hard on the coffee. There was a mêlée of handshakes and air-kissing. Florence pressed Kate's hand. Stevens bowed graciously, and said quietly, away from the others, "Norman tells me you're his best officer. Will I see you at the Goodwin boy's funeral?"

"Someone from the team will be there to pay our

respects," replied Kate.

Stevens nodded and turned back to the others.

"Well, Kate, what do you think?" said Fordyce beaming as they approached the car.

"I think I had better drive, sir," said Kate holding out her hand for the keys.

"Norman, please," replied Fordyce. "The evening's not over."

"It is for me, sir," said Kate, reaching for and taking the keys. "I'll drive you home and I'll get a taxi from there."

Nothing was said on the way back. Fordyce sulked as a chocoholic might on dipping his hand into the box and finding nothing there.

43

Alice laid her head on Wyatt's shoulder. They were on the settee holding hands, both looking into a dreamy distance.

Wyatt said, "I think I was beaten up as a warning. But warning me of what?"

"To keep away," replied Alice.

"To keep away from Brett?" queried Wyatt. "If that's the case, it suggests he doesn't want to be found, or they don't want him found."

"They don't particularly sound like friends," said Alice. "Also, I don't get the link with pubs and restaurants. He was a car dealer."

"Dealer!" said Wyatt, suddenly enthused. "Maybe that's it. He was dealing something else."

"You mean like drugs!" exclaimed Alice.

"That or something else. I saw the same people coming and going out of the two places I visited. They could easily have been delivering or collecting something. I thought it strange at the time, but now it makes sense."

"We have no idea where he is or what he's involved in, so maybe it's time we reported him missing. It doesn't look like he's going to come back," said Alice.

At that moment, as if on cue, the doorbell rang. Wyatt and Alice looked at each other, alarmed.

"I'll answer it," said Alice. "Just in case."

A moment later she returned.

"Tom," she faltered. "It's for you."

From behind Alice stepped a wiry, diminutive figure, dressed in black with a face that could cut through ice.

"Sister Angela!" exclaimed Wyatt, non-plussed. "What are you doing here?"

"I'm here to tell you, Father Wyatt, that your mother has been taken ill and she would like to see you," said Sister Angela evenly. "I would have called but you don't appear to be answering your phone."

"It's broken," said Wyatt, lamely. "But how did you know where to find me?"

"As you well know, Father, God sees everything," replied Sister Angela, then added, "and Mrs. McGinty lives over the road. Expect an audience with His Grace the Bishop when you return. Good evening, Father." And to Alice, "I'll see myself out Mrs...."

"Miss Green," said Alice.

"Miss Green," Sister Angela confirmed and looked hard at her as Medusa might have looked upon a mortal and, for a moment, it seemed that Alice had indeed turned to stone.

Wyatt, too, was stunned. It took a moment for him to shuffle his thoughts and try to find clarity, floundering like someone trying to find the exit in a smoke-filled room.

Alice's face was white; her eyes were glazed; it was as though the mirror that was herself had cracked and splintered into a thousand shards.

Wyatt spoke first. "Alice, I will have to go. I'll be in touch." He went to her and held her close. "I will be back."

Alice nodded, her head against his shoulder. She held on as a shipwrecked sailor might to flotsam, willing it to be strong enough to endure in a stormy and treacherous sea.

44

The Royal Oak in Upper Chittle was a former coaching inn in what at one time must have been a bustling settlement. Behind the church opposite was a castle mound, early Norman. Adjacent to the church was a former tithe barn, long since converted into a row of three terraced cottages. To the side of the through road ran a stream. Some of the street names suggested its past activities: Cattle Drove End; Horsefair; Tanner's Lane; as did the names of the houses: The Old Forge; Mill House, Cordwainers; Sheepfold.

The significance of Upper Chittle declined as nearby towns grew and the distances between them were shortened by time. There was still a faint echo of its trading past in its twice daily bus service, but now it was a village and, like many in the Cotswolds, exuded charm, tranquillity and comfort.

Lee Thompson drove through the arch to enter the car park of The Royal Oak. He was out to celebrate. He'd just been offered a new job, with plenty of extra money promised on the side. His debts had been cleared. He could see a way out from his insufferable mother. So what if Levinson had warned him, had told him to clean his act, he was not an addict, not some crazy cokehead; he was an occasional user, like a social drinker, so there was no harm in that and definitely no reason not to celebrate.

He chose The Royal Oak because he knew the

landlord pretty well but in reality he could have gone virtually anywhere. It was as easy to score coke in a pub as it was to buy sliced bread from a corner shop. Not that every landlord was a dealer, far from it, but there wouldn't be a village that didn't have its users, and a village pub was a natural meeting place. Pubs were social places, dealing was a social activity and taking blow made you feel good. Dealing was discreet, taking it was private. Pubs were perfect.

Thompson entered the bar. An open log fire blazed in the hearth; warm light glowed from brass lamps; a black and white cat was curled up in a Windsor chair; a canoodling couple occupied a high settle.

"Half a lager, please, mate and a ..." Thompson drew his right index finger under his nose.

The barman nodded. A moment later he returned with the glass. Thompson handed over a fifty pound note and felt the press of a small package in his palm. He turned from the bar to take a seat by the window. There was no change to wait for. He leant back and took a deep swig before heading off to the toilets.

45

The collation board for Ritchie Goodwin still looked sparse.

"How are you getting on, Sergeant?" said Kate to Benson.

"Very slow, ma'am. Constable Turner is still working through phone video footage. It's like looking for gold dust in a sand dune. I've been looking into his background and there seems nothing there. Good lad, nice family."

"Write up all the businesses George Stevens owns and the names of the key people who work for him. I can give you Thompson and Thompson Estate Agents, principal partner Johnny Thompson, our esteemed mayor; also Town and Country Motors, manager Brett Barron. He hasn't turned up for work but not officially a missing person. And while you're at it you might as well put up Jim Curtis, manager of Three Counties Bank."

"You can't think there's a conspiracy writ large involving the great and good in the community," said Benson.

"No, but I'm told Stevens is convinced Ritchie was on to something. I keep hearing the word family. Well sometimes families fall out. Sometimes big time."

Benson wrote the information on the board.

"It's the boy's funeral this afternoon," said Kate.

"Yes, ma'am. Constable Turner and I were going to pay our respects. Might be interesting to see who turns up. A chance to see what the family's like," said Benson.

"Sergeant, I know tact isn't your strong suit, but do tread carefully. Stevens and the others are mates of Fordyce, and I wouldn't like you to stymie what's left of your career."

"I'll tread as carefully as a blind man in a field of cowpats," quipped Benson.

Kate smiled, "It won't be me cleaning your boots."

"Ma'am?" asked Sheldon.

"Yes, Joe."

"Did your visit give us more to go on?"

"Not a lot but there may be an army connection with drugs going back a long way that may be worth exploring. These two are dead," Kate said pointing at the photograph, "but this one," she continued, tapping the figure of Jock McAndrew, "is very much alive. We should see him."

Sheldon wrote army and McAndrew's name up on the board. Kate looked at what was there. It wasn't the time, if there ever would be, to let anyone know about Martin.

46

The crematorium was set about half a mile off the main road heading out of town. It was approached by a tree-lined drive which headed gently downhill until opening out to a small plateau overlooking a patchwork of fields.

Benson and Turner waited in their car until the small group at the door had gone inside, then walked in briskly to take a seat at the back.

Ritchie's mother sat at the front being comforted by relatives and close friends. The service card indicated that the eulogy was to be presented by George Stevens.

Benson nudged Turner, tapped the card and said, "Handy. I'll have a word with him after."

They looked around.

"Do you recognise anyone?" asked Turner.

"The chubby guy with the smug face, three rows up, is the mayor, Johnny Thompson. He's just nodded to the chap on the other side. The sharp dresser. Thin face. Don't know him."

"Maybe connected to one of the businesses the Inspector mentioned," suggested Turner.

"More than likely," said Benson.

The service had been allotted half an hour but was over within twenty minutes. There was little that was particularly religious about it. A crematorium official acted as emcee and two popular ballads from the late nineties took the place of hymns.

Benson whispered to Turner, "I want Queen's *Another One Bites the Dust* at mine."

Turner's hand shot to her mouth to suppress a giggle.

The high point of the service was the eulogy by George Stevens. He spoke eloquently and movingly about Ritchie. Ritchie was clearly someone he knew well and was attached to. To Benson, the grief seemed genuine as was that expressed by the mother and others in the front row. He looked to Thompson and the others. They were solemn but distant; one or two were beginning to fidget. To him, they seemed to be there, like himself, out of duty rather than respect.

A moment after the curtain closed around the coffin the emcee attended the door to the front right and stood head bowed while the congregation waited for Mrs. Goodwin to lead the way out to the small courtyard beyond.

Benson and Turner were the last to leave and, in the courtyard, introduced themselves while shaking Mrs. Goodwin's hand. Mrs. Goodwin looked tearfully at them in turn. "Please find who did this, who took my boy from me."

"We will, Mrs. Goodwin. We will," replied Benson

and, for the first time in a long time, there was no doubt or cynicism in his mind.

Mrs. Goodwin turned away to be comforted by those closest to her. Benson caught Stevens' eye and, with a sense of mutual intention, they made their way towards each other.

Benson began, "Detective Sergeant Benson, Detective Constable Turner. We're in the investigation team. I must say Mr. Stevens that was a wonderful eulogy you gave."

Stevens shook their hands. "He was a wonderful boy. Almost like a son. Have you got far with the investigation?"

"We're following certain lines of enquiry. Very early days but we're hoping for a breakthrough soon." Benson hoped that the uninformative clichéd response would suffice.

"That means you have nothing," said Stevens.

He was about to turn away when Benson said, "I understand you may be following your own lines."

Stevens stopped, taken aback, "How would you know that, Sergeant?"

"We are detectives Mr. Stevens. It's our job to find out things. If you know anything we should know, you need to tell us. It would be helpful, too, to have a list of the names, addresses and telephone numbers of all your employees and those in your associated companies."

"I'm beginning to like you, Sergeant," said Stevens. "I'll email a list first thing tomorrow. Oh, and one other thing."

"I think you are just about to remind me of Brett Barron," said Benson.

"Impressive, Sergeant. Very impressive," said Stevens, with a firm nod of the head. "Are you a mind reader?"

"No, sir, but I do read reports."

"So he's being treated seriously as a missing person?"

"We treat everything seriously, sir, even missing cats," was Benson's deadpan reply.

Stevens turned away and headed over to a small group which included Johnny Thompson and the thin-faced man. Benson took out his phone and discreetly took a photograph of the group.

"Sergeant," said Turner, "is that allowed?"

"Watch and learn, Constable, watch and learn," replied Benson, slipping his phone in to his pocket as they headed off back to their car.

47

"D.S. Sheldon", Sheldon answered. "You're kidding. I'll be right there." He replaced the phone and turned to Kate. "Ma'am, have a guess who's just turned up at the front desk?"

"The lady from the Premium Bonds with a big cheque in her hands?" offered Kate.

"Better than that ma'am. Cindy Graham," beamed Sheldon.

"Well, Joe, bring her in. Let's see what she can tell us."

Cindy Graham looked careworn, but not downtrodden. Her face was lined and slightly puffy; there was the faint yellowing of a fading bruise under her right eye. There was nothing stylish about the way she dressed.

"We've been looking for you," began Kate. "Do you know about Geordie?"

"That's why I'm here. My sister heard something on the news. I came back to see the boys. They said you'd been round."

"What do you know about the circumstances of his death?"

"Nothing. He was shot, I think," said Cindy.

"Assassinated would be more accurate. Who do you

think would do that and why?"

Cindy shook her head. "He was always the wide boy. He wouldn't tell me anything, but I knew that café was dodgy. He couldn't have been making any money frying bacon and pouring tea. He had plenty of cash to flash, not on me and the boys, mind, so something was wrong."

"What do you think he was up to?" asked Kate.

"You're the detective, but even a blind man could see it must have been drugs."

"You knew he was dealing?" asked Sheldon.

"Guessed. Using and dealing," replied Cindy.

"He didn't treat you well," said Kate, changing the direction.

"No, he was a bastard. That's why I left. Had enough of him and that shitty place. I'd lost the boys. There was nothing to stay for."

"Just coincidence, then. You leaving and him being killed," added Sheldon.

"I wished him dead a thousand times but I didn't kill him," said Cindy.

"Or arrange to have him killed?" continued Sheldon.

Cindy looked at Sheldon as if he was a completely bald man who had just gone into Toni and Guy's and asked for the full shampoo and set. "And how would I do that?"

Kate smiled to herself and redirected, "Did he ever mention any names?"

"No."

"Your boys said I could borrow this photo," said Kate producing the picture she had taken from the house. "What can you tell me about the people on it?"

"Oh yes. The army. His mates," she sighed deeply. It was as though she was looking backward through a telescope to a time long gone. "It was good for a while. He spoke about it sometimes. There were some capers, he said and these seemed to be at the heart of everything."

"Do you know their names?" asked Kate.

"Can't remember them all. I think he said one or two had died, but that one there," she said pointing, "is Jock."

"Jock?" questioned Kate, expecting a surname.

"Dunno. But when he used to speak to me, he spoke about Jock a lot. I think he respected him rather than liked him. No, not respect exactly," she corrected herself, "more like fear. I got the impression Jock was the leader of that little gang."

"Did he ever talk about particular things they did? About their tours to Afghanistan, maybe about their officers?" Kate's heart was palpitating. She was almost afraid to hear a stranger mention Martin's name.

Cindy shook her head. "I could tell when he got back once that something must have happened but he was too shocked or scared to talk about it."

"And officers?" ventured Kate.

Cindy shrugged. "No. Geordie had no time for them. Thought they were all educated donkeys."

Kate nodded, and felt oddly relieved. "Do you know if Geordie kept in touch with Jock?"

"A while back I do remember him mentioning his name and that they were meeting up or planning to do something."

"To do with drugs?" asked Kate.

Cindy shrugged, "Who knows?" Then as if realising something for the first time, "Are you saying that Jock might have killed him?"

"I'm not saying, Mrs. Graham. You said Geordie feared him. You just put a thought in my mind. Geordie might have upset someone he feared."

He was certainly very good at upsetting people," confirmed Cindy. And then, as if there was nothing more to say, she added, "When can I have his body for burial?"

"It should be released in a day or two. Somebody will be in touch," said Kate rising.

With a determination in her eyes, Cindy looked at Kate, "He might have been a violent, feckless bastard, but he was my violent, feckless bastard."

"If we need to speak further, where will you be?" said

Sheldon.

"At home with the boys," Cindy replied. "Now Geordie's gone, it might not be too late." But there was no conviction in her voice, and Kate's eyes offered no hope.

As Joe was escorting her to the door, he said, almost as an afterthought, "By the way Mrs. Graham, did you ever hear Geordie mention the name of Bazzer?"

"Bazzer?" she repeated and thought. "He might have meant Brett Barron. He bought a car off him once."

Sheldon looked to Kate. Kate looked at the white board at the far end and back to her own. She sat down momentarily stunned. "Sergeant Benson," she called.

"Yes, ma'am."

"Clear a space here, then bring your board down and put it next to mine. Looks like our cases are connected and we're all going to be working together."

"Goodoh," said Benson, "I like a party."

"That's good because you're going to have to put up the decorations. I want all that info rearranged with George Stevens' name and companies in the middle at the top. I'll be back in half an hour. Got some googling to do." Kate got up and strode purposefully to the door.

48

"Reprographics," said a female voice.

"D.S. Sheldon here. I left some paperwork with you for copying and attaching to the file for Crime Number 11637, stolen picture frame, con man on Summer Heights. Victim, a Mr. Wentworth."

"All done. The originals are in a brown envelope at the front desk awaiting collection."

It was a dark and dreary day. Addison Street looked as if it had been washed with grey. All colour seemed to have faded from the cars, the houses and the few people shuffling along the pavement.

Sheldon was not going to bring much warmth and light to Mr. Wentworth as he knocked on the door and waited. He knocked again.

"Coming," grumbled a voice. "Hold your horses."

The door opened. Wentworth was in his wheelchair but looked more crumpled than Sheldon remembered from his previous visit. A few days' growth of stubble, unkempt hair, a food-stained cardigan, and urine-stained trousers gave Sheldon the impression that Wentworth had given up. The lively aggression he had witnessed in his voice at the first meeting had given way to resignation. Wentworth turned and made his way into the sitting room. Sheldon followed.

"D.S. Sheldon," said Sheldon. "I'm returning your insurance documents. I'm sorry to say the frame has not turned up." He handed over the envelope.

Sheldon looked around and realised what it was that had struck him as being so odd on his first visit. There were no other pictures or photographs in the room – not on the walls, on the shelves, on the side or by the television.

"I know the frame was very important to you. The file is still open so if we get anything we'll contact you straight away."

"Bugger the frame," said Wentworth, in a sudden outburst. "It's the picture I'm missing. The only one I've got and the only one to remember by." He sighed heavily as though he was going to sob but didn't have the energy or had forgotten how to. "And now he's dead..." Wentworth's voice trailed off.

"I'm sorry to hear that," said Sheldon. Then, struck by a sudden idea, he said, "There's a photograph of the frame and picture in the envelope you have. You could get a blow-up to replace the original. It's amazing what you can do these days. Not expensive, either."

A look approaching gratitude and hope appeared on Wentworth's face as he opened the envelope and drew out the contents. He shuffled the papers, placed the photograph on top and showed it to Sheldon. The Victorian frame looked solid, expensive and heavily elegant. But what stunned Sheldon was the picture, for inside the frame in clear focus was the beaming face of younger Geordie Graham.

"That's Geordie Graham, isn't it?" said Sheldon, surprised and a little confused. "Geordie Graham's your son?" he said, trying to find understanding.

"Stepson," said Wentworth. He came with his mother God rest her soul. He was a good lad really. I tried to bring him up as my own, but you know what it's like."

Sheldon nodded, although he had no idea.

"They go their own way," Wentworth continued. "And now he's dead. That picture reminds me of the happiness of the past and what might have been. It's the only one I've got. All the rest, lost, gone, destroyed."

"Do you know the circumstances of his death?" ventured Sheldon.

"I've been told. I'm not surprised. He was always into something. Look around this estate, mate, what wouldn't you do to get out?"

"He joined the army, didn't he?" said Sheldon.

"Yes. Should have been the making of him, but in the end he wanted to escape from that too."

"Did he ever talk about those days?" asked Sheldon.

"A bit, but he was cagey. He made some good mates though. Used to talk a lot about them."

"Anyone in particular."

"The name I heard most often was Jock."

"Jock McAndrew?" asked Sheldon. Wentworth nodded. "Was he still in contact do you know?"

"Dunno." Wentworth looked again at the picture. " Geordie used to come round every so often and leave me a few quid if he was flush. He was a good lad at heart, but I kept the picture not because it was him, but because it reminded me of his mother. I hope you catch the bastard who nicked it."

"It's still an active case," said Sheldon.

"You say it's easy to get a copy?" said Wentworth.

"Next time you get into town, ask in Boots. Someone there should be able to help you."

Wentworth turned his wheelchair away in a gesture of hopelessness. It was as though 'town' was a black hole and Boots was a distant planet being sucked into it.

Sheldon closed the door behind him and left Wentworth to his memories.

On the way back to the station another thought suggested itself. He would run it past Kate to see if there was any mileage in it.

49

Levinson studied the chessboard. Spassky v. Fischer, Reykavik, 1972. The white knight was pressing. He moved the black bishop as a countermeasure. Barron's phone should be easy to obtain, he thought. If the priest hadn't got it, then it must be at the apartment. It wouldn't be long, too, before Barron would be reported missing and, once the police were involved, it might be a little more difficult to get the phone.

He sat in his car on Bullpit Lane. He noticed a fast-moving red mini approach and suddenly come to a halt with a screech of rubber. A diminutive female figure, dressed in black, emerged and marched purposefully to the door of number fifteen. She was let in. A few minutes later she emerged, got into the mini and sped off along the street.

Less than ten minutes after that, a male, mid-thirties, came out, bag in hand. He looked uncertain, reluctant perhaps, like a man without a map at an unmarked crossroads, having to make a choice but not daring to. He turned and gently touched the face of the female standing in the doorway. They embraced. Levinson knew who she was – Barron's piece of skirt. The other must be the priest. The scene reminded him of parting lovers so often portrayed in the black and white films of the nineteen-forties. So touching, he thought, wryly. Looks like she's bared more than her soul to him. The man got into an old blue Golf and drove off. Levinson waited ten more minutes then left.

The following morning at seven o'clock, Levinson was parked in the same position. There was no blue Golf in evidence. Just after eight, Barron's ex appeared. She looked dressed for work. She had a handbag over her shoulder and a shopping bag with what looked like buff manila folders inside. She looked drawn and despondent but nevertheless headed off purposefully down the street towards the main road.

Levinson waited ten minutes. He'd noticed the way the door had opened and closed. The lock was straightforward. He drew out a wrap of cloth from his pocket, opened it and selected two picks. He pulled a cap over his head. He looked around. The coast was clear. He strode over to the door and within a few seconds he was inside. To an observer, it would have looked like he was the keyholder: his confidence, speed and skill creating the illusion of permission.

He scanned the sitting room. There was no reason for the phone to be hidden. He took out his own phone and tapped in Barron's number. He heard a ring tone coming from the kitchen. He saw the phone on the worktop next to the microwave. He cut the call, picked up the phone, put it in his pocket and left. He scanned the street: no cars, no pedestrians. He got in his car and set off. He smiled to himself. He was relaxed. The niggle had faded.

Only the Almighty would have noticed the barely perceptible settling of the curtains in the house opposite.

50

The united team was looking at the collation board.

"Nice decorations, Sergeant," said Kate, nodding to Benson, who accepted the compliment by nodding sagely in return. "What else have we got to bring to the party?"

Sheldon and Benson began to speak at the same time. "Sergeant Benson first," said Kate.

"I have these ma'am," said Benson, producing clear head shots of some of the principals who had attended the funeral, and attaching them to the board.

"Good, Sergeant. That's Stevens. And this one," said Kate tapping the board, "is Paul Levinson, manager of The Black Cat. And this, Johnny Thompson, mayor and estate agent."

"I also have this," said Benson, brandishing a sheet of paper. "Just received this morning. A list of names, addresses and contact details of all staff employed in Stevens' companies, courtesy of Mr. Stevens himself."

"Very useful, Sergeant," said Kate.

"More than useful, ma'am," replied Benson, knowingly. "Informative."

The others looked at him and waited a moment for the dramatic revelation. When they all had that 'go on then' look on their faces, Benson continued, "Sherlock downstairs has confirmed that the call to Geordie Graham's phone from Bazzer came from the phone owned by Brett Barron."

"Which means?" asked Kate.

Ideas began to tumble out.

"That Bazzer is Barron and Geordie knew him well. Called him by a nickname," offered Sheldon.

"That Barron's disappearance may be connected to Geordie," said Benson, "and to Ritchie Goodwin. Barron seems to have disappeared just after the stabbing."

"Good," encouraged Kate. "More thoughts?"

"That Barron didn't kill Geordie," said Turner.

The others turned to her. "Explain," said Kate.

"Because, ma'am, the call came in after we found Geordie dead. Why would you call someone if you know they're dead?"

They all nodded in approval.

"That they had a shared interest," offered Sheldon. "Was it to do with Barron's business or Geordie's?"

"Was it drug-related, then?" added Turner.

"Whatever the connection, and we are in guessing territory here, there is too much to ignore," said Kate.

"You asked me, ma'am, to see what I could find out about drug distribution," said Sheldon. It's a complicated picture but it's thought that Avonmouth is the main point of entry. There, consignments are sub-divided to go to retailers, as it were. These retailers develop their own networks and so on down the chain until it ends up in tiny packages in pubs, clubs, gyms, schoolyards and street corners."

"So, looking at this board, what do you think?" asked Kate. Again the energy was palpable.

"The quantity of drugs found at Geordie's café suggests he's a big retailer, a sub-wholesaler," Sheldon offered. "Perfect place to distribute. Your customers come to you."

"And," added Benson, "this might be obvious but cars are transport. They can pick up and deliver."

"And The Black Cat's a night club. Perfect final distribution outlet," added Turner.

"And Mr. Stevens is a very rich man and lives in a big house," said Benson.

"And there's another big fish," said Kate, tapping the picture, "and that is Jock McAndrew. Not too much on record, minor misdemeanours as a juvenile, but a bit of googling brought up a picture and a biography. He's running an extensive import/export business out of, you've guessed it, Avonmouth. Sergeant Benson and Constable Turner, note the relevant stuff on the board and see what you can find out about Barron. Sergeant Sheldon and I are going Bristol way to see what Jock McAndrew can give us. Good work Ian and Fiona."

Constable Turner blushed with pride and, old hand that he was and a few months off retirement, even Benson was warmed by the use of his first name.

"Before we go, I've got one odd thing. Maybe something or nothing," said Sheldon.

"And that is?" said Kate.

"We had a report of a conman on Summer Heights masquerading as a utilities worker. A valuable picture frame was stolen." The group was looking quizzical, seeking the relevance. "But the odd thing is," continued Sheldon, "the picture inside the frame was of Geordie Graham." The group became alert, brows deepened. "The chap who had his frame stolen was Geordie's stepdad, the only link he had to his late wife."

"Ideas, anyone?" said Kate.

"Was it a spate of thefts?" asked Turner.

"No, only this one reported," replied Sheldon. After a moment's reflection, he continued,. "It might seem daft ma'am, but maybe it was the photo that was the target not the frame."

"But why would someone do that?" asked Turner.

"Identification," said Kate.

"To pass on to a hitman," added Benson.

"Or because you are the hitman," said Sheldon.

"One way or the other," Kate concluded, "if we can find the conman we might be one step closer to solving this. Well done, Joe. I think we are beginning to see shapes coming out of the fog."

After the team had left, Superintendent Fordyce emerged from his office and looked closely at the board. He scratched his head as if trying to find something, like a springtime squirrel looking for the nuts it had hidden in a lawn the previous autumn.

51

"Well, Constable, what do you think?" said Benson.

"I think we try Town and Country Motors first."

"Why?"

"Because if he's disappeared there's not likely to be anyone at home. At work we might get something to go on."

Benson nodded. "You're getting good at this. You can drive."

Turner pulled up just outside the office of Town and Country Motors.

"I'm sorry, you can't park there," the woman behind the reception desk said. "Reserved for deliveries, and I'm expecting one now."

"Oh, I think we can," said Benson, showing his card and bending down to look closely at the badge on her chest, "Sharon." His smile was passive-aggressive.

"Oh," Sharon replied, a little flustered. "How can I help?"

"We're looking for Brett Barron."

"Who isn't?" Sharon replied. "Mr. Stevens wants to

know where he is. I want to know where he is, and there was a chap here the other day wanting to know where he is."

"And who would that be?" asked Turner, growing in confidence.

"No idea," replied Sharon. "Said he was a friend looking for him."

"Not by chance anyone on this photo?" said Benson showing the picture of the army pals.

Sharon shook her head.

"Any reason you can think of why he would just take off and leave?"

Again, Sharon shook her head.

"Was he a good manager?" asked Turner.

"Yeah, alright. We have a steady business here. Customers seem to like us. They keep coming back."

"How are you managing without him?"

Sharon rolled her eyes and lowered her voice. "Got a new manager. Now. Young bloke. Fancies himself. Thinks he knows it all, but knows nothing. Lee Thompson, the mayor's son," she tutted.

At that moment Lee Thompson appeared from the door that led to the workshop.

"Ah, Mr. Thompson," Sharon said. "The police are

here asking about Mr. Barron."

"Well you won't find him here," said Thompson. "Last month's sales figures, if you don't mind, Sharon. Soon as you can." Without waiting for the acknowledgement, he turned and went to the inner office.

"I see what you mean," said Benson to Sharon. "You can also tell him when you take him the sales figures that Barron may well not be here, but that won't stop us looking."

A hint of a smile broke out on Sharon's face as the two officers departed.

"The son of the mayor put in as manager. How does that strike you, Constable?" asked Benson.

"Cosy, close-knit, like a family, as the inspector said."

"Like bloody incest to me," retorted Benson. "If there's not something rotten going on there, I'm a Dutchman's uncle."

"You don't look like a Papa Smurf to me," said Turner, kindly. "Apart from the big blue nose and the whiskery chin, that is."

Benson guffawed. "Next stop, Bullpit Lane. Let's see if anyone's at home. You can do the talking. You've got all the wisecracks. I want to see the extent of your repertoire." Benson shook his head and guffawed once more.

***

Constable Turner knocked on the door of 15 Bullpit Lane. She wasn't expecting anyone to come to the door, and no-one did. "We could try later," she said to Benson.

As they turned to leave, Benson caught a glimpse of a curtain settling in the house opposite.

"I suppose we'd better go back to the station and keep looking through the camera footage," said Turner.

"Maybe, but first let's see what Papa Smurf can discover. Follow me."

Turner looked quizzical as she followed him over the road and knocked on the door of the house opposite.

A small wizened woman with close-permed grey hair and dark eyes behind blue plastic-rimmed spectacles came to the door and rather nervously said,"Yes?"

"Good morning, madam, I'm Detective Sergeant Benson, and this is Detective Constable Turner," Benson said, showing his ID. "I wonder if you might be able to help Mrs..."

"McGinty," she replied.

"We're trying to contact Mr. Brett Barron. He lives over the road. Do you know him?"

"I know who he is, but I don't know him."

"Have you seen him recently?" asked Benson.

"No, I don't think he's there anymore. I thought you were going to ask about the gentlemen callers," she said, knowingly.

Benson and Turner looked at her questioningly. They knew they were being played for dramatic effect, so waited.

"Well, she must be a right one," continued Mrs. McGinty. "Her a teacher as well. Lakeside Comprehensive. No sooner than one gone than another appears. And I shouldn't probably say this, but he was a priest."

Benson and Turner looked at each other and wondered if they were listening to someone who had lost the plot, or maybe had found one between the covers of *The People's Friend*.

"And then again", Mrs. McGinty continued, "only this morning someone else turns up, lets himself in and out as if he owns the place."

"Sounds like a regular Piccadilly Circus," said Benson. "Did you recognise this last one?"

"No."

"And the woman is...?" asked Turner.

"Alice Green. I don't know what to think. She seemed such a nice girl."

"That's been very helpful, Mrs. McGinty. We won't keep you longer. Don't get cold," said Benson, and with that they returned to their car.

"Well?" said Benson.

"Save me from curtain twitchers," said Turner.

"Don't dismiss them, Constable. Curtain twitchers are a treasure. They are a storehouse of information. They are like unpaid informants and, if you can cut through the gossip and prejudice you might find a nugget of pure gold."

"And have we struck gold here, Sarge?"

"Not yet maybe. But we keep digging. Let's go to school. We might learn something there."

Benson laughed at his pun. Turner shook her head at its corniness. As they set off, Mrs. McGinty's curtain settled once more.

***

It was break time as Benson and Turner drew up in the car park of Lakeside Comprehensive. Two adolescent boys strolled by the car, eyes and heads darting left and right like bluetits on a garden feeder. One produced a packet of cigarettes, flipped the lid and offered it to the other.

"Bad for your health, lads," said Benson, winding down the car window.

The boys quickened their pace as they headed towards the ornamental shrubbery fronting the road.

"Takes me back. Happy days," said Benson. "Ten to one those lads think they have found the perfect smoking den. One to ten on the teachers know exactly where it is."

A plume of blue smoke rose gently from the shrubbery. As Benson and Turner entered reception, a middle-aged man with the gait of a sergeant-major and the instinct of a shark smelling blood was heading through the car park to the bushes.

Two minutes after asking if they might see her, Alice Green, pale and nervous, was sitting in the visitors' room opposite two police officers.

"We're looking for Brett Barron," began Turner. "He's been reported missing by his employer, Mr. George Stevens."

Alice looked completely bewildered. Thoughts swirled in her head. She had absolutely no idea how to begin so she said simply, "So are we."

"We?" asked Turner.

"A friend and myself," she replied, and for clarification, "Father Thomas Wyatt."

Turner and Benson nodded together as if having a fact confirmed.

"How long has he been missing?" asked Turner.

"Since Friday. We had an argument. I walked out. When I came back he was gone. I haven't seen him since."

"And the argument was about?" Turner's tone was sympathetic.

"Everything...us...his behaviour...his lateness... his playing around." Alice's mouth tightened.

"The last straw, then," suggested Benson.

Alice nodded.

"You didn't report him missing, but you were worried enough to try to find him," queried Turner.

"We thought he was with his friends," Alice said. "I wanted the relationship over. I wanted him out, to clear his things. I didn't want him coming back."

"Any luck?" asked Turner.

"No. We tried his work. We found his phone and tried a few numbers off that but no luck," replied Alice.

"Curious," said Benson. "Why wouldn't he take his phone with him? The phone is most people's most vital organ after their heart."

"I wondered that," said Alice.

"Do you have the phone with you?" asked Benson.

"No, it's at home," replied Alice.

"Do you think you could take the rest of the morning off and come with us to pick up the phone?"

"I think that can be arranged. But why do you want his phone?" asked Alice.

"For the same reason you did. To see if we can trace him."

"But why do you want to find him?" said Alice.

"He might be able to help us with other enquiries,"

said Benson.

Alice nodded, the light of understanding flickered. She thought about what Wyatt had experienced on his day trip to Bristol. "Drugs?" she ventured.

Benson and Turner looked at each other, eyebrows raised in interest.

"And why would you say that, Miss Green?" asked Benson.

"I'll explain when we get to my house. It'll make more sense when we have the phone."

In the car park the two smokers, red-faced, heads bowed, were walking slowly ahead of the sharkish sergeant-major figure like condemned prisoners on the way to the scaffold.

Benson wound down the window and addressed the boys. "I did tell you, lads, that smoking was bad for your health." He wound up the window and said to Turner and Alice, "It may be a school but some things kids never learn."

***

"That's strange," said Alice. "I thought it was in the kitchen." She moved a fruit bowl and utensil holder, looked around then started rummaging through drawers.

"Perhaps you could try the number from your own phone," suggested Turner.

Alice took out her phone and tapped. There was no ring, no redirection. "Dead," she said. "I don't understand it. I'm sure the phone was here."

"Does anyone else have keys to your flat?" asked Benson.

"No, why," replied Alice.

"Father Wyatt?" suggested Turner.

"No. Why do you ask?" repeated Alice.

"Because," said Benson, "according to your neighbour over the road..."

"Mrs. McGinty, the eyes of the Lord," interjected Alice.

"...you had a visitor this morning. A man."

Alice looked puzzled. "I don't understand. Are you saying someone's broken into my flat and..."

"Taken the phone," concluded Turner. "Looks like."

"But why?" insisted Alice.

"Because of what's on it," said Benson. "You say you tried some of the contacts. What can you recall?"

"What was odd was that the contact list is full of nicknames or names in code."

"Can you remember any?" asked Turner.

"Well mine was Imp. I remember one was Cawdor."

"Cawdor? Could you spell that, please?" asked Turner, noting them.

"C.A.W.D.O.R. A character in **Macbeth**. A traitor. Another was Flipper. One was Bitch. I can't recall any more. Oh, some were places. Anchor."

"How do you know they were places," said Benson.

"Because Father Wyatt went to a couple. In Bristol and..." Alice hesitated.

"And?"

"And someone beat him up."

Turner and Benson looked at each other. "Why?" said Turner.

"We think as a warning. He noticed the same people coming and going. We thought maybe they were delivering drugs or something."

"You didn't report it?"

"No. I think he felt ashamed. Not sure what he was getting into."

"And where's Father Wyatt now?" asked Benson.

"Carlisle. His mother was taken ill. I don't know when to expect him back."

"Tell him that we will probably need to see him. And we may need to see you again. If you can think of anything else, let us know." Benson handed over a card. "I suggest you change your locks. Something more substantial. I don't suppose whoever it is will be back, but just to be safe."

Alice nodded. After the officers had left, she sat down heavily. She felt lonely and afraid. She wished that Tom was there and she was being held tightly in the comfort of his arms.

***

"Well, what do you make of all that, Constable?" said Benson, as they were driving back to the station.

"I think we may have one answer and a few more questions," replied Turner.

"Okay, Mastermind," said Benson. "Let's have the answer first."

"Miss Green seems honest and her story hangs together. If they were looking for Barron and using his phone that would answer the question of who called Geordie's phone after he was dead."

Benson nodded. "And questions?"

"I was thinking about what you and the boss said at the office."

"Which was?" asked Benson.

"The boss said the photograph of Geordie Graham was stolen so he could be identified. Maybe Barron's phone was stolen to prevent identification. Could it be the same person? If it is, it would mean that whoever it was knew Geordie well enough to know where his stepdad lived, and know Barron well enough to have a nickname. So if I'm right we're looking for someone who knew them both well."

"Not bad. I see the way you're thinking," acknowledged Benson. "But you have put a dark thought in my head."

"Which is, Sarge?"

"Why would someone steal Barron's phone unless they knew he wasn't able to collect it himself. And why wouldn't he be able to get it himself?"

"Because he's disappeared," said Turner.

"Because he's dead," replied Benson. "And that might mean we have three murders on our hands."

They drove on, mulling over the consequences of their thinking. At a traffic light, while they were waiting for the change to green, Benson said, "You said there was something I said at the office that made you think."

"Yes, Sarge. You said cars were good for delivering drugs. The priest went to an address in Barron's phone and was beaten up for nosing around. Might be drugs, he thought. That's another link between Barron and Geordie. Maybe we need another visit to the garage."

"There's time enough for that, Constable. We don't want to lose sight of Ritchie Goodwin. So back to the office, a few notes on the board for the boss to mull over, then back to checking the video footage. But I want to say, Constable, you'll make a good detective. You've got good instincts."

"Thank you, Sarge," said Turner, blushing.

"May be when I go, you'll be good enough to fill my boots."

"Looking at the size of those dusty clodhoppers, that's going to be a very difficult thing for my dainty feet to do."

They drove on silently in the warm glow of mutual admiration and respect.

52

To remain a competitive, world-class trading centre, Bristol had to have bigger, more accessible docks. Ideally placed for trade across the Atlantic and into the Mediterranean, from Scandinavia to Africa, Bristol knew it could have the edge over Liverpool if it expanded, so the city's Victorian, entrepreneurial forebears looked towards the river mouth. What they started has continued. Container traffic is a twenty-four hour operation, as is the pumping of oil and conveyance of grain in and out of huge storage vessels and silos. The constant shunting of trains under the giant legs of derricks and cranes, the sound of horns, the kaleidoscope of lights create the sense of a busy, dehumanised city. The tower blocks are made of containers and the streets between them inhabited by forklift trucks.

The Avonmouth Trading Company consisted of a small office block and two huge warehouses situated on one of the many trading estates that had grown up and sprawled over reclaimed land within a mile or more of the docks. It was easy to find but not so easy to gain access. The perimeter was bounded by heavy duty fencing and the entrance was via a gatehouse.

"Looks like a fortress," said Sheldon, drawing up behind a container lorry to wait in turn.

"Must be something valuable inside," said Kate.

Eventually, with an exchange of paper, the lorry in

front rolled into the compound. The uniformed gatekeeper leaned out of his window. "Yes?" he enquired.

"We're here to see Mr. McAndrew," said Sheldon, showing his ID.

"Is he expecting you? said the gatekeeper, checking his screen. "Can't see anything here."

"No, but he will want to see us," said Kate.

"Just a minute," said the gatekeeper. He picked up a phone and dialled a number. "A couple of police officers are here to see Mr. McAndrew." He waited a moment. "Okay, right." then he leaned towards Sheldon. "Spud, here, will escort you."

A tall uniformed guard with eyes like pinholes and a face like a potato emerged from the office. He was smartly dressed in tie and collared shirt, not quite high enough to cover a couple of tattooed stars on his neck.

"Follow me," he said. He walked in front of the car and led the way as an undertaker might lead a funeral cortège. After crossing the compound, he pointed to a space for the car to park. He waited for the officers to get out then walked towards an office door. He entered. Kate and Sheldon followed.

The reception area was surprisingly light and spacious. The first impression was of stainless steel furniture and abundant foliage. A photograph might have made it look like a rather exotic greenhouse, but there was no stifling humidity. There was a freshness, almost a wholesomeness about it. On the walls were hung colourful photographs of exotic fruits, each one perfectly focused and true-to-life, but suggestive of sexual organs, both male and female. Depending on your state of mind you might think you were at Kew Gardens or in a high class brothel.

"These people are here to see Mr. McAndrew," said Potatoface to a young receptionist with black hair and a low neckline. He gestured for the officers to move forward. When they did, he stepped behind them and stood like a sentry at the door.

Kate leaned towards Sheldon. "I think we're here on their terms now, Joe."

A buzz sounded. The receptionist said, "Mr. McAndrew will see you now." She stood up and held open a door to the side. Kate and Sheldon walked past her into the office.

They recognised Jock McAndrew immediately. His features had thickened, his hair had thinned, but in essence it was the same squat ginger-haired toughie they knew from the photograph, though in the picture he looked freckled, now in the flesh he looked as if his face had been pebble-dashed with pea gravel.

He was behind a desk. He didn't stand up but he gestured for the officers to sit. Sheldon looked around and brought over two chairs. It was clear whose territory they were in and who was directing operations.

Kate introduced herself and Sheldon. "Mr. McAndrew," began Kate.

"Call me, Jock," said McAndrew. His voice was as

thick as tar and his Glaswegian accent sounded like surf pulling back on a shingle beach.

"Mr. McAndrew," said Kate, accepting that the struggle for power had begun, "we're investigating the death of Geordie Graham and we are hoping you may be able to help."

McAndrew shrugged, opened his arms as a priest might in celebrating mass, but not in sanctity, in expectation of an explanation.

"You do know, Geordie?" asked Kate.

"Yes. But why ask a question you know the answer to? I've nothing to hide. We served in the army at the same time," replied McAndrew.

"And you know he's dead," continued Kate.

"Yes. Word travels, especially amongst old army pals," replied McAndrew.

"We suspect he was the victim of a professional hit," said Kate.

"And what has that got to do with me?" replied McAndrew. He picked a pencil out of a holder. He began to run his fingers along it as though counting the beads on a rosary.

"We suspect the motive might have been drugs. Cocaine to be more precise," said Kate.

"Again, what's that to do with me?" replied

McAndrew, calmly stroking the pencil.

Kate let the question hang in the air.

"You have a good business here, Mr. McAndrew. At least it seems busy. What do you do?"

"Import, export. You may have noticed we're near docks. That's what happens near docks."

"Thank you, Mr. McAndrew. I'm learning something. And you import?"

"Fruit and vegetables, mainly from South America, USA, Caribbean and South Africa. We're the big wholesaler. We redistribute to the big supermarkets and smaller wholesalers. If you had a banana today, the chances are it came through here." There was hint of tough pride in his voice.

"And you export?"

"Whatever. You can't send a ship back empty. Agricultural machinery, computers, medical equipment, chemicals, stuff like that. But you haven't come here for a lesson in economic geography. So, how can I help?"

"Cocaine is imported. Geordie was found in possession of a substantial amount. You know Geordie and you run an import business with connections to South America," said Kate. "I was wondering if you could shed some light on why he was killed and who might have arranged it."

McAndrew smiled but there was no warmth in the

expression. "You are on a fishing expedition, Inspector. Be careful of the waters. There may be sharks in it." McAndrew dangled the pencil and bobbed it like a float. "I'm sorry I can't help." There was a pause. "Mathematics is not your strong point is it, Inspector? You seem to have added two and two and arrived at five. You need to go back to school. You're looking in the wrong place. Geordie was always a risk-taker. Looks like he took one risk too far."

"Probability theory is an established branch of mathematics, Mr McAndrew."

"Then you will know that this meeting has probably run its course," said McAndrew, tapping the pencil against his teeth.

"There is one other thing you might be able to help with," said Kate, producing the photograph of the army pals and handing it over.

McAndrew took the photograph, studied it hard and handed it back. "Ah, the good old days," he said.

"I wonder if we might talk about them. In private," said Kate.

Sheldon perked up and looked quizzical. "Ma'am?"

McAndrew was intrigued by the request and the reaction. He pressed his desk phone. "Louise, send Spud in." He turned to Kate. "We have a busy and legitimate business here. We have nothing to hide. Your colleague might like a guided tour."

The security guard who had escorted them earlier came in.

"Spud, give this Detective Sergeant a guided tour, top to bottom. If he fancies a banana, pineapple or passion fruit, let him have one. Don't forget to show him the separation department and the chill rooms."

The guard nodded and turned. Sheldon got up and followed. There was something about the tone that suggested the tour was not going to be an altogether enjoyable experience.

The moment the door closed, Kate began, "For the moment, I accept you may or may not know anything about the circumstances of Geordie's death or about the import and distribution of cocaine into the south west but, those things apart, we have something in common."

"We like fruit and vegetables," suggested McAndrew.

"Or rather someone," continued Kate. McAndrew leaned forward, interested. "Captain Martin Brown."

McAndrew nodded his head in recognition. "A good man, Inspector. Tragic end. And your interest?"

"He was my husband," said Kate.

"I see," said McAndrew, interested and surprised. "And your interest in Geordie has taken you back. Must be awkward for you. Inspector, when the private and professional collide."

"I can keep them separate," said Kate. "I'm interested

to hear you say Martin was a good man. What did you mean?"

"He was a good officer. Led by example. Real guts. Got us out of a scrape in Kajacki once. I could say I'm here today because of him," McAndrew said with the firmness of truth.

"You could also say you're here today because he's not here today," responded Kate.

"Explain," said McAndrew, tapping the pencil against his teeth.

"It's taken a long time but I have a very clear picture now of the circumstances of Martin's death. I know what you were up to, and I have a good idea Martin knew what you were involved in. It wouldn't have been long before your heroin smuggling enterprise was uncovered. You would have been facing criminal charges and a long custodial sentence. If Martin hadn't died, I don't think you would be here now."

"Captain Brown's death was unfortunate. I don't wish to be harsh but every cloud…"

"You say unfortunate. I say deliberate," said Kate. "I'm here to tell you that when the professional and the private collide, as you put it, the private takes priority." Kate looked steadily and determinedly into McAndrew's eyes.

"Your implied threats are misplaced," said McAndrew. "Let's accept that what you say about my enterprise is true. Captain Brown was doing his job. He was a man of courage and integrity. I would expect him to try to do his job well. For me it was part of the risk. Any businessman knows that. Just the same for you and the people you meet in your line of work. If Captain Brown had anything on us, it couldn't have been much. Most of us left soon afterwards, honourably discharged. No, Inspector, Captain Brown wasn't killed because he was onto my sideline. He died at the hands of the Taliban defending our position."

"Is that what you really believe?" said Kate.

"No reason not to," said McAndrew. "It was all a bit messy one way or the other. We heard nothing to the contrary though the attack did put an end to business. But, that's life."

"You'd be surprised to learn then that Martin and his interpreter were killed, shot in the back by bullets from a standard British Army issue L85 assault rifle," said Kate.

McAndrew looked genuinely stunned. He took a deep intake of breath. Momentarily his neck seemed to swell and his pupils dilate. He leaned forward. "Few things surprise me, Inspector, but that has." He tapped the pencil on his desk. "You know that for sure?"

"As close to official as I'm going to get," said Kate.

There was a moment's pause. McAndrew doodled hard, straight lines on the pad in front of him.

"That photograph you have in your pocket, Inspector, take it out and look at it." Kate took out the photograph. "What do you see," said McAndrew.

"A group of army pals, only one of whom is alive."

"So the question I would ask myself, Inspector, is not who is in the picture but who is not in the picture."

Then it came to Kate in an epiphany, a road-to-Damascus moment, a jolt of insight, like a shaft of light breaking through a dense cloud. "Who took the picture?" she asked.

"Levinson. Lance Corporal Paul Levinson."

The effect was immediate. She exhaled. "Thank you, Mr. McAndrew."

"Though we might see the world differently, we're not dissimilar, you and I," said McAndrew. "We believe in justice."

"Are you in contact with him?" asked Kate.

"Let's just say I know where he is and I know what he's capable of," replied McAndrew. He tapped the pencil against his teeth and looked deeply into Kate's eyes. "I said earlier Geordie was a chancer. He might have wanted to do things differently, perhaps branch out on his own. He could have upset someone that way." He paused, allowing time for thought. "I don't usually ask for the personal numbers of police officers who come knocking on the door but, in this case, I wonder if you would mind leaving me yours." He took the pencil from his mouth and pushed it with a notepad across the desk.

Kate looked at the pad then up to the pebbledash of a face and deep into the greenness of the eyes beyond. They held each other's gaze.

"Justice, you say."

"Yes. Justice," replied McAndrew.

Kate picked up the pencil and wrote her personal number on the pad and pushed it back across the desk.

"Just in case," McAndrew said, "I have anything for you. You never know." He tapped the pencil twice on the desk and, in a gesture of finality, put it back into the desk-tidy.

There was a knock at the door. In walked the security guard with Sheldon.

"Excellent timing. We're all done here. I trust you enjoyed the tour, Sergeant," said McAndrew.

"Thank you, sir. Enlightening." Sheldon looked to Kate to gauge any cause for concern, but saw none.

Kate stood.

"Forgive me if I don't shake hands, Inspector, we have very strict health and safety regulations here," said McAndrew.

Kate smiled. "No problem, Mr McAndrew." She knew the comment was not aimed at her but was for the benefit of both Sheldon and the security guard. McAndrew, after all, had a reputation to maintain. "We all have our standards."

"Very true, Inspector. Escort them to the gate, Spud."

As they were weaving their way back to the motorway

through a seemingly endless sequence of roundabouts and traffic lights, Sheldon said, "If you don't mind me asking, why the private chat, ma'am?"

"Call it nous. I could tell I was likely to get more if the situation seemed less formal," said Kate.

Sheldon was not wholly convinced but said, "And did you?"

"Yes," said Kate. "He gave me Levinson's name. They were in the army together."

"Levinson!" exclaimed Sheldon. "So that makes a direct link between Geordie and Ritchie Goodwin."

"Yes," said Kate. "Too much of a coincidence to ignore. Let's see if we can shine more light on him," and as she said it she hoped that beam was strong enough to reach back over the years.

53

"Celia," said Johnny Thompson. "Come into my office. Now." He put down the phone. He was fidgeting; he was on edge; he couldn't settle. His face was still round and ruddy, but it wore the look of a battered beachball, abandoned on the beach at the mercy of the wind and tide. He didn't know whether to open a filing cabinet or turn on his computer; he didn't know whether to sit down or stand up; he was caught between action and inaction, and he could control neither. He was out of his depth; he was floundering; he was in a panic; he needed help.

"Celia," he said, as a bespectacled woman, late fifties, trim, firm and calming entered. She had the air of a kindly, grandmotherly, no-nonsense primary school teacher. Her presence soothed; waters calmed and wind lessened as she said, "Yes, Mr. Thompson."

"Celia, I need help sorting out the files and accounts for the last ten years, maybe longer. I don't know where to begin."

"May I ask why?" said Celia, with an authority that demanded truth.

"Mr. Stevens will be scrutinising the transactions. I just want to ensure that everything is in order," replied Thompson.

"Then I suggest we begin with those in which you had

a direct personal interest," said Celia.

"Thank you, Celia. I'm going out now to clear my head. Perhaps you could make a start." As he headed out of the door, he turned. "I don't know what I would do without you, Celia."

"Drown, probably," said Celia, as the door closed and she opened the top drawer of the filing cabinet.

54

"Take a seat please, George," said Jim Curtis ushering Stevens into his office. The contrast between the bank manager's office and the banking hall was enormous.

The banking hall was a huge space, largely devoid of people, both customers and staff. It was akin to a bright and glossy supermarket where customers would help themselves to services. The machines and automatic counters attached to the walls were intended to be self-explanatory so even the most challenged of readers would be able to know how to withdraw money, pay bills, deposit a cheque, buy some euros or dollars. Questions were discouraged. If you had a query it would be difficult to know how or where to find an answer. You would have to approach a machine and play it like a Las Vegas slot. After a while you might hit the jackpot. If not, you would have to head to the town centre for a coffee and to plan the next strategy.

Jim Curtis's office was oak-panelled, a nod to the heritage of the Victorian building in which the bank was housed. On the walls were framed old cheques and share certificates from a bygone age, together with turn-of-the-twentieth century white five pound notes. The office conveyed trust, probity and confidence, unlike Jim Curtis whose usual ebullience had evaporated and left a man in spiritual torment.

"You asked me to look into the businesses in which you have an interest, and the personal dealings of those who work for you," said Curtis, clarifying his remit.

"That's right, Jim and you've called me to make me aware of things I know or should know," replied Stevens calmly.

Beads of perspiration were breaking out on Curtis's brow. "You will assure me, George that what I share with you will be held in the strictest confidence."

"Of course. You have my word," said Stevens, whose presence and tone suggested the solidity and permanence of granite.

Curtis cleared his throat. "So far, I've only been able to look into the estate agency accounts and Johnny Thompson's private account. The news is not encouraging."

"Go on," said Stevens.

"Whilst most of the transactions are above board, there are some which involve Johnny directly. Over the years there have been a number of properties which he has acquired in his own name or the names of his son and wife. The properties were purchased through finance provided by the agency, so properly should be in the name of the owners, that is, you and Thompson."

Stevens' face began to darken. "Go on."

"Later, the properties were effectively assigned to him through guarantee, so to all intents and purposes, they are his alone. Also the properties themselves look as if they have been acquired through dubious means or, rather, sharp practice. Many look as though they are the result of executor sales. Johnny would value the property for an estate, convince the executors that the valuation was the market value, tell the executors he has a firm cash buyer on his books. The executors, only too happy to discharge their duties, quickly agree to the sale. Johnny ends up with the property." Curtis leaned back, a little smug, as if he had been a lawyer presenting an unchallengeable case in the High Court.

"And the deeds to these properties are where?" asked Stevens.

"Here," said Curtis. He bent down and lifted a pile of manila folders. "Johnny left them here for safekeeping. I've had them brought up from the strongroom."

"What would you say is the current valuation?" asked Stevens.

"About three million pounds."

"So, in short, Thompson has lined his pockets at my expense. He has defrauded me. Whilst at the same time gambling with my integrity. If any of these practices come to light then, as co-owner of the estate agents. I could be held criminally liable."

"That's what it looks like," said Curtis.

Stevens sat still. He was brooding. Deep within his being, the spirits of his ancestors stirred. Aine, the Celtic goddess of revenge and Nemesis, the Greek goddess of retribution appeared out of the mists of antiquity. They saw each other in each other. In Stevens' imagination they formed and bonded and coalesced. The power, the desire was immense but like an alchemical reaction the red furnace of anger transmuted into a river of cold steel. Vengeance would be his.

"There is also this," said Curtis, leaning down, then placing a safety deposit box on the desk. "It's in Johnny's name. I don't have a key."

"I do," said Stevens. He drew the box towards him. He felt in his pocket and took out a Swiss army knife and selected the strongest pick.

"George! You can't do that!"

"Oh, I can. And you've described how everything is at least part mine."

Stevens forced the lock. The lid sprang back to reveal tightly rolled wads of cash, sterling and euros.

"A nice little nest egg," said Stevens. "Now what are we going to do with the cuckoo?"

Curtis wiped his brow. He looked pale and clueless. He had no idea how he would begin to explain to the bank inspectors on their next visit.

Stevens said, "I'll wait for your secretary to draw up transfer documents for everything here, Jim. Don't worry. You'll get the signed papers in due course."

As Curtis left the room, Stevens wondered if it was

this discovery that had cost Ritchie Goodwin his life.

55

Fortunately, Mrs. Wyatt's heart palpitations were not as serious as she or her neighbour had thought so, after a comfortable stay over, and with many hugs and assurances, Wyatt found himself making the long journey back. Music had to be faced, so he had phoned ahead to book an audience with the bishop. He was expecting a tough examination.

The Bishop's Palace was bigger in name than in actuality. The name suggested size, power, authority and antiquity but was, in fact, a nineteen sixties executive house built on some land behind the cathedral. A Morris Minor parked on the drive, suggested a knowing humility, though Wyatt knew that for official engagements, the bishop took advantage of a chauffeur-driven Lexus.

The bishop was an avuncular-looking man who wore a broad smile and steel-rimmed spectacles. He was tall and had a ponderous gait. He might have been taken for a gentle hippopotamus but his reputation was one of a cross between a wily fox and a ferocious alligator.

"Take a seat, Father," the bishop said, pointing to a chair in front of a large, red, leather-topped desk, behind which he sat with his elbows firmly implanted and his finger tips splayed and pressed against each other.

Wyatt sat down.

The bishop looked at Wyatt and waited. He held

Wyatt's gaze and waited still. It seemed for a moment to Wyatt like two gunfighters on the dusty street of a Western town, each waiting for the other to make the first move.

Wyatt spoke first, "I'm here to offer my resignation, your Grace."

The bishop continued to look hard at Wyatt. He waited. It was as though he was studying him, noting his posture, his slightest movements, the steadiness of his hands, the blinking of his eyes, the moisture on his brow, as a poker player might look for a tell in his opponent.

"Which I accept," the bishop said. "You have one week to tidy up any personal parish matters, after which time you will be required to leave the presbytery. You will be given a grant to cover living expenses for three months, after which you will be on your own. I will, of course, furnish you with supportive references for any job you might apply for. Call in to see Sister Angela at the Diocesan Office on your way. You'll find your resignation letter ready to sign. I think that covers it. Good day, Father."

Wyatt stood, nodded a head bow, "Your Grace", turned and left the room.

Outside, Wyatt took a deep breath. He'd expected a grilling, to be challenged on his actions and his faith, to be persuaded against resignation. He felt for a moment quite giddy, as though he was both free and in limbo. He exhaled sharply and headed towards the Diocesan Office where coming face to face with Sister Angela promised a far more daunting challenge.

ABSOLUTION

In his office, the bishop, having accepted the inevitable, was doing some calculations. The world was changing; church attendances were falling; priests were haemorrhaging; seminaries were closing; the traditional Irish supply lines were trickling into nothing. West Africa was still flourishing, however, but the bishop wondered how well Senegalese curates with heavy French accents would go down in the Cotswolds. He was too much of a rationalist to accept the trite aphorisms that miracles happen or that God moves in mysterious ways, but as a churchman he had faith, and with faith came hope.

56

"I trust, Lee, you are getting to grips with the motor trade." said Levinson over the phone.

"Yes, Mr. Levinson," replied Thompson.

"Good. You will have noticed you have a three year old white Kia Sportage on your books. It's in the showroom with a 'sold' ticket on the windscreen.

"Yes, Mr. Levinson."

"You will bring it now and park it behind The Black Cat. You will leave it for half an hour, then you will take it down to the Bristol Car Auctions for this afternoon's auction. You will attend the auction. Another car will be bought on your behalf. Listen out for lot number 201 then follow instructions. Inside the car there will be some addressed packages. You will deliver those packages as directed and collect another in return. Your final stop will be where you started. You will leave the keys in the car and walk away. You will collect the car in the morning, valet it, put it in the showroom window and slap a sold sticker on it. Have you got that?"

"Yes, Mr. Levinson."

"It is easy, straightforward. Do not deviate from the plan. Do not be curious. For your efforts you will be handsomely rewarded. You will be expected to save, invest and live within the means of a salesman manager. Do that, and you can expect to have a bright future and be a very wealthy man. However, if there is any indication that you're unable to follow the instructions or draw attention to yourself by your behaviour, the consequences will be very serious. Understand?"

"Yes, Mr. Levinson."

The call ended.

Thompson went to the front office, opened the cabinet and riffled through the keys until he found what he wanted.

"Sharon," he said, "I'm off to the auctions."

"Righto, Mr. Thompson. See you tomorrow," said Sharon, relieved.

Thompson drove the Kia out of the showroom. He dismissed the implied threat. His focus was on the comfort of the future. Levinson, in his clarity, certainty and strength, gave him confidence. He knew that by following simple instructions all would be well. He turned on the radio, tuned into a country music station and set off. He was going to enjoy his jaunt to the west.

***

Levinson put the phone down and went over to study the current game. Black was in an unassailable position. There was clearly no way out for white. One, two or three moves down the line would make no difference. Levinson smiled and tipped over the white king. Order had been restored. He picked up the pieces and reset the board. He thought he might have a look at Kasparov v. Topalov and see what he could learn there.

57

It had only been a few days earlier when Johnny Thompson was driving his black Discovery up the tree-lined avenue of Highfield looking forward to a day's shooting. Then, he had the expectation of good sport and jolly banter. Today he didn't know what to expect, and that troubled him. He couldn't refuse George's invitation to discuss a business proposition, but George had given no details so he felt unprepared and at a disadvantage.

He scrunched to a halt, checked his face in the mirror, shook his jowls to relax, ran his hand through his hair, straightened his tie, gulped and made his way to the front door.

"George is expecting you," said Florence. "Go on through to the library."

Perhaps it was George Stevens' cultural heritage that taught him never to underestimate the power of theatre. As Thompson entered the library he stopped, puzzled.

George Stevens' desk was set into the bay window. Behind the desk, with his back to the view beyond, sat Stevens. On the desk was an array of items: a brace of pheasants, a shotgun, a fillet knife, a haunch of venison, a riding crop, a mantrap, a walking stick with a bone handle and a box of rat poison. In the middle of these was a pile of files and folders, title deeds and other legal-looking papers. Bank notes, held tight by elastic bands, stood in neat cylinders. All was arranged with a sense of care and balance, as though an artist was about to paint a still life.

"Good of you to come, Johnny. Don't stand there. Do take a seat." Stevens gestured to the Windsor chair which faced the desk.

Thompson approached and sat down nervously. Stevens came from around his desk. "Johnny, do rest your arms on the chair," said Stevens softly. "That's it. Good." Stevens took a cable tie from his pocket and attached Thompson's left wrist to the arm of the chair.

Thompson's eyes flicked backwards and forwards to Stevens and the items on the desk. "No need to worry, Johnny. Just a little restraint in case you get too excited and want to leave before we've finished."

Thompson's mouth was dry. He could find no words to utter. He sat, startled. He tried to move his left wrist, where he could see the skin was already whitening.

"Have you ever taken the breast out of a pheasant?" asked Stevens. Thompson shook his head. "No? Then let me show you." Stevens picked up a fillet knife and drew a pheasant to him. "First of all, feel through the feathers to locate the skin just under the crop. Then make a little nick with the knife. Now with both hands tear the skin which will part just like tissue paper to expose the breasts. Do you see, Johnny?" Thompson nodded. "Press back the legs then, with the tip of the blade follow the line of breast bone and rib cage all the way round, down, along and back to where you started." Stevens produced a neat cut and held out the breast. "Perfect for the freezer or the oven. In fact, I might have that for supper this evening."

Stevens approached Thompson and ran the tip of the knife, down Thompson's nose and on to his chest. "The secret to a good cut, Johnny is a good knife. Don't you agree?"

Thompson nodded. Sweat was forming on his forehead.

"Let me show you this," said Stevens, pointing to the mantrap. "I have several of these in the cellars. According to the estate records, the last time one of these was used was in 1929. I expect some hungry soul was after a deer, or making his way to the lake. In any event he never walked in a straight line again."

Stevens picked up the haunch of venison and placed it on the release plate. The iron jaws snapped together with the sound first of the dull creak and scrape of metal on metal, then the crunch of mighty teeth through bone. The force of the movement caused the trap to jump, lift its prey a few inches in the air, and land with a dull thud back on the desk. The flesh on the haunch was crudely torn, the bones were crushed and splintered.

"Crude, but effective," said Stevens. "You do have to be so careful when you go into the woods. Don't you agree, Johnny?"

Thompson wiped his brow with his right sleeve. "Yes, George," he managed to say, his voice squeaking.

"Of course, on an estate like this we enjoy our sport, as you well know," said Stevens picking up the shotgun, inserting two cartridges, snapping it shut and moving it around as if following a target, until it rested pointing directly at Thompson's head. "But, sadly, accidents happen." Stevens pulled the trigger. A loud report shook the room. Thompson flinched and squeaked. "Oh dear. Blanks. How fortunate!" said Stevens, breaching the gun and laying it back on the desk. "Alas, too, we have vermin." Stevens picked up the riding crop and tapped the box of rat poison. "And vermin have to be controlled. Don't you agree?"

"Yes, George," replied Thompson. He looked pleadingly at Stevens, then lowered his eyes.

"Rats die an excruciating death. They can't resist this stuff. They drag it back to their nests for the family to enjoy but soon after they start eating it their throats and stomachs begin to burn; they start haemorrhaging; they get into a mental frenzy and expire. It's not a quick death but it is effective. You would think the species might have learned to avoid this delicacy, but that's nature I suppose. Some things cannot be resisted or learned. It has the same effect on human beings. That's why there are warnings all over the box. It has to be handled with care."

Stevens cracked the riding crop on the desk. The sound was like a pistol shot. Thompson jerked in his seat and looked at Stevens.

"But I haven't invited you here today to talk about country matters. You're here so we can discuss these," said Stevens tapping the riding crop on the files and rolls of money. "Now, where shall we begin?"

"Let me explain," said Thompson feebly, his squeaky

voice turning to a whimper.

"I think the time for explanation is over, Johnny. I have the full picture. Celia was very helpful when I called in. She had the files all ready for me. And Jim Curtis was most forthcoming."

Thompson gulped and looked around in desperation. He tried to stand but the cable tie held him fast and he sat back awkwardly in the chair. It was as though he had been caught in the act, with his trousers down, playing with himself on a crowded beach. He realised there was nothing he could say, so he said nothing and looked at the floor.

Stevens selected a folder and opened it. "Mmm. Very nice, Johnny. A seafront property in Marbella. Bit hot for me in summer, but lovely in January, I'm told." He selected another. "A Georgian town house, converted into a Greek restaurant, popular location. The rental income is impressively lucrative." Stevens picked up another folder but discarded it. "I could go on, Johnny but you get the picture. All of these," he tapped the pile with the riding crop, " are the result of your fraud and deceit. You have defrauded me. You have jeopardised my own integrity and, more than that," Stevens walked around Thompson, brought his face close to his, "you have betrayed my trust."

Stevens' voice was as cold as iced steel, but his arm moved rapidly. Thompson felt the riding crop brush his hair and crack on the back of the Windsor chair. Thompson flinched and screwed his eyes.

"And for that, Johnny, there is a price." Stevens picked a pen from the holder on his desk, held it out and said,

"You will sign these papers."

Too stunned to do otherwise, Thompson took the pen with his free hand and signed the proffered sheets. "What are these?" squeaked Thompson.

"These are transfer documents, authorities, legal entities, what-you-will which put all of your properties, assets, business interests and so on into my ownership. All with immediate effect."

"But..." Thompson spluttered,

"I am not a completely heartless man, Johnny, so what will remain to you is your house, your car and five hundred pounds in your bank account. Very reasonable in the circumstances."

Stevens took out his Swiss army knife and cut the cable tie.

"And now, Johnny, you are free to go. You will never, ever come to this house again." Stevens pointed to the bloody and shattered haunch. "Trespassers will be dealt with."

To himself as much as to Stevens, Thompson muttered, "But I'm the mayor. What will my wife say? What shall I do?"

"You have a house. You were an estate agent. I'm sure you can think of something."

Stevens took the bone-handled walking stick from the desk, flicked it to indicate Thompson should move to the door, as a shepherd might to a dog.

"Florence. Mr. Thompson is leaving. He won't be coming back."

Stevens returned to his desk to tidy away the props. His brows furrowed as he wondered whether there was any truth in the adage *like father like son*, and decided to investigate further.

58

"So, Inspector, how may I help? Are you getting any further with finding Ritchie's killer?" said Levinson, leaning back in his chair, relaxed and confident.

"Small steps," said Kate. "I'm hoping you can help us with another matter."

"Which is?" replied Levinson.

"This," said Kate, handing over the picture of the army friends.

Levinson looked at the picture. He looked at Sheldon, then Kate. "I'm sorry, I don't understand"

"What don't you understand, Mr Levinson?" said Kate.

Levinson became tetchy. "I don't understand what the other matter is you wish to talk about."

"Do you know these people, Mr Levinson?"

"Why do you want to know?"

"Because we are investigating a serious crime. Again, do you know these people?"

"Yes," replied Levinson.

"How? In what capacity? said Kate.

"We served in the army together."

"That wasn't so hard, Mr. Levinson. I think we would make better progress if you would just be a little more forthcoming. Surely, you have nothing to hide."

Sheldon could feel the atmosphere becoming tense. It was like witnessing two stags about to lock antlers.

Levinson drew a breath to regroup. He felt he was about to expose his king so he castled for protection.

"I'm sorry, Inspector. Of course. This Ritchie business has rather rattled me." He looked at the photo again. "Yes, they were the good days. Sadly, they've all gone bar one."

Kate looked to Sheldon. Levinson looked to them both.

"Is that why you're here?"

Kate and Sheldon waited for Levinson to supply an answer to his own question.

"Geordie Graham. I'd heard he'd passed away."

"How did you hear that?" asked Kate.

"Word gets around amongst old pals," said Levinson.

Kate had heard the same phrase recently. "You mean from Jock McAndrew?"

"Possibly. The army's a big family," said Levinson.

"Then you'll know Geordie was murdered.

Assassinated," said Kate.

"That's unfortunate," replied Levinson. "But I'm not sure how I can help?"

"When was the last time you saw Geordie?" asked Kate.

"We kept in casual touch but I haven't seen him for months," replied Levinson.

"Did you have any business dealings with him?" asked Kate.

"Business? No. I understand he had a transport café. We've got nothing in common."

"Not drugs?" ventured Kate.

"I don't know what you mean," said Levinson, shifting in the chair.

"I wondered if there might have been a link between the past and the present," said Kate.

"Go on," said Levinson, hesitantly.

"There are only two of you left, and I'm not just talking generally about your little gang here, but from the last time you were all in action together. You remember the incident at the forward operating base that precipitated the departure of you all from the army?"

Levinson readjusted himself in his chair. He took a tissue from a box on his desk and wiped his hands.

"I'm not sure I can help you there, Inspector. I've tried to erase the memories of those times. But you seem well-informed."

"I am, Mr. Levinson. Very well informed," replied Kate. "It's almost as though I was there myself." Kate left the cryptic remark hanging in the air, then said, "Do you know Brett Barron?"

Levinson shook his head, non-plussed, trying to make sense of the question, where it was leading and how to respond. He tried to look thoughtful. "Brett Barron?"

"Yes, Brett Barron, manager of Town and Country Motors. Last time I was here you said you knew people in Mr. Stevens' businesses. Well, Brett Barron is one of those."

"I probably do, then," said Levinson. "But what about it?"

He's gone missing. Disappeared," said Kate.

"I'm sorry. I can't help," said Levinson. "If there's nothing else, Inspector, I must get on."

Kate and Sheldon rose to leave. At the door, Kate turned. "You know, Mr. Levinson, it's probably coincidence but you do seem to be very close to a lot of death and disappearance."

Left alone, Levinson walked to the chess board. He looked at it then, suddenly overtaken with an uncontrollable urge, he raised his fist and smashed it into the board. The pieces scattered. The white queen rolled towards his foot. He raised his leg and stamped it. The queen remained unbroken. It was made of granite.

***

Outside, Sheldon turned to Kate. "What was all that about, ma'am?"

"I think Benson and Turner are on to something, suggesting the connection between Geordie and Barron. The links may be tenuous, but they're getting stronger. Levinson is a common thread," said Kate, not wishing to add more to the certainty she felt. "Sometimes, Joe, detection is like playing cat and mouse. Levinson might think that because the club is so named, he is the cat. But he knows and we know there are too many coincidences. He's going to have to scurry quickly if he's to avoid our claws."

59

"I think these will smooth your worried brow, Jim," said George Stevens, passing over the signed authorities allowing access to Johnny Thompson's accounts, securities and safety deposit box.

Jim Curtis sat back, relieved. "I've looked closely at the transactions of Town and Country Motors and The Black Cat but I can see nothing to cause suspicion."

"What about the personal accounts of Paul Levinson and Brett Barron?" asked Stevens.

"Levinson has a current account and small deposit account. Salary cheque and usual outgoings. Nothing unusual. Looks dead straight," said Curtis, "But Barron's has more irregular movements. Occasional deposits of large amounts of cash, sudden withdrawals. Then, there is this," Curtis leaned to one side, picked up a small safety deposit box and put it on his desk. "Shall we take a look?" he suggested.

"I thought that was against your principles," said Stevens.

"Of course, I wouldn't normally, but this is the cheapest box on the market and over time you collect keys from old, damaged boxes, desks and so on." Curtis opened the desk drawer and drew out a bunch of small keys. He shook them and smiled at Stevens, conspiratorially. "I'm sure one of these will fit, and I shall lock it up after. No one except us will be the wiser."

He jiggled the keys for a while then the box opened. He looked inside and pushed the box over to Stevens. "Well, well. What's this?"

Inside the box were a number of sealable, clear plastic packets, each containing a white powdery substance. Stevens picked out one and examined it. Each looked from the packet to the box to each other, and both at the same time exclaimed, "Drugs!"

"Better wipe that packet and put it back," suggested Curtis.

Stevens nodded, wiped the packet clean and replaced it.

"What shall we do?" said Curtis.

"The only thing you can do," replied Stevens. "Lock the box, wipe it clean and put it back in the strongroom."

"Shouldn't we tell the police?" said Curtis.

"And you risk losing your job for unauthorised access to a customer's safety deposit box. I don't think so. Put it back, Jim and say nothing. You are sure," Stevens said, rising to leave, "that there is nothing odd about Town and Country Motors."

"All looks perfectly normal, financially. Good turnover, healthy business," said Curtis.

"All the same, this," Stevens said pointing to the box,

"suggests not all is right."

He wondered for the second time in recent days whether this had something to do with what Ritchie Goodwin was going to tell him.

60

"I'll be moving out in a few days," said Lee Thompson, breaking the long silence.

"That's good," said Johnny Thompson, but there was no enthusiasm in his voice.

Elaine Thompson said nothing. She was sitting at the breakfast table, head bowed, face drawn, picking at a slice of overdone toast. Suddenly, she stood up, the chair scraping back on the tiled floor, and spoke in a voice, taut with tension, "I still don't understand it Johnny. We have to sell up?"

"Yes, dear. I should have told you before, but business is in a bad way and I'm afraid everything is gone. Just the house left. We can't afford it. It'll have to go."

"But my garden?" she said, unable to accept the enormity of the change ahead.

"Oh for God's sake," said Lee. "Shut up about the bloody garden. Get a life."

She looked at her son and her husband. Their images cracked and blurred as tears came to her eyes. She shook in disbelief and sorrow for a moment, then turned and made her way to the garden.

"I might be able to help out, Dad, if you're stuck," said Lee, smugly. "I've got a nice little earner."

"You be careful, son. Stevens is sniffing around. He did for me. He'll do for you," said Johnny.

"The man's a fool. Anyway, he won't find anything wrong with Town and Country Motors. All legit," said Lee.

At that moment from the garden came a high piercing scream. A pause. Then the scream continued. Johnny started and began to rise from the table. Lee pressed him back into the seat. "I wouldn't bother. She's probably just found the cat. I stuffed the old fleabag just behind the rhododendron. I was going to bury it, but so what. It had a quick death. A quick cut with the kitchen knife. Still, she can always stick it in a box and take it with her."

Ashen-faced, drained of energy, Johnny looked at Lee and in his eyes saw his own reflection.

"I'm off to work," said Lee. "Things to do."

61

The props had been tidied away. The library felt cosy and homely. It was a place for business but it was also a place of security. George Stevens sat at his desk, the early Spring sunshine warmed his back. In front of him in the Windsor chair sat Paul Levinson, relaxed and listening.

"It seems you're the only one I can trust, Paul. It's not the money. It's the disloyalty, the betrayal that hurts most. I think it was that that Ritchie was on to. If only he had spoken earlier," said Stevens.

"A tragic loss," uttered Levinson.

"Johnny Thompson, I am delighted to say, has had his come-uppance but, despite my earlier confidence and your recommendation, I wonder if his son is actually the right person to run Town and Country Motors," said Stevens.

"I had no reason to doubt him, but then I had no reason to doubt his father," said Levinson.

"Quite," replied Stevens. "What's worrying me is Barron's involvement. I have very good reason to believe he's dealing in drugs."

Levinson sat up and leant forward. "Drugs? How so?"

"I won't tell you precisely but a good quantity has been found in his name. The fact that he has disappeared seems to confirm it. Again, I feel my trust has been betrayed. I always thought myself a good judge of character," Stevens sighed, "but now my real concern is not with him but how his dealings might have involved the company. If the company is implicated then by association I am implicated." With his voice steadily rising, Stevens said, "I am my name. I am my reputation." He brought his fist down hard on the desk. The stationary holder rattled and the bell mechanism inside the vintage telephone dinged.

"I understand," said Levinson, evenly.

"Barron has taken off for a reason. I've looked closely at the books of Town and Country but can find nothing out of place. I want to make sure that the business is not involved in any way in illegal activities. So this is where I need your help, Paul," said Stevens.

"I'll do whatever you want, Mr. Stevens," said Levinson.

"You know how to run a business well. You also know Lee Thompson. I'm going to put you in as mentor to him. I want you to scrutinise him and the business. I want to find out if Barron has been using my company in any way for his nefarious activities. Can you do that, Paul?"

"I'll do my very best. Thank you for your confidence, Mr. Stevens," replied Levinson.

As the front door closed behind him, Florence turned to George. "There is something about the way he looks and moves that reminds me of a fox. What was it that Caesar said about Cassius. He has a lean and hungry look. Such men are dangerous. Are you sure you can trust him?"

"Absolutely, my dear. That is experience, strength and determination you see there. He's the only one I can trust to help me. He'll get things done, and I know my confidence will be repaid. Do you know, I feel better than I have done for a long time. Let's go and think about a holiday. I have just acquired a lovely place in Marbella that's worth a visit."

Stevens took Florence by the arm and headed to the heart of the house.

***

A broad smile broke out on Levinson's face as he drove down Highfields' tree-lined drive. What looked as though it might be a problem was, in fact, a solution. He would go back and reset the chessboard. Sometimes, even under the most challenging of circumstances, fate or your opponent will play into your hands.

62

With the absence of Tom and after the visit by the police, the bubble of self-delusion in which Alice had wrapped herself burst. With Tom's optimism and certainty and her feelings for him, she had allowed herself to believe that Brett Barron was still alive, but she knew, because she had killed him, that he was dead.

She couldn't account for the absence of the body, nor for the stealing of the phone, nor for the police's interest in him, other than that they must be connected in some way. She hadn't been completely honest with the police and that was beginning to worry her.

The one thing that she was certain of was, whatever the future held, Brett Barron was no longer a part of it, so it was with a sense of heart-heavy determination that she began to gather Brett's belongings to dispose of either at a charity shop or the local tip.

She felt both awkward and afraid, guilty and righteous by turn as she checked the pockets of his shirts and trousers, jackets and coats. In turn, she folded each one and placed it as neatly as possible until the black bin liners were filled. She didn't know whether the charity shop would love her or loathe her when she dropped off the numerous bags as she intended to do later that week.

She was beginning to feel a sense of accomplishment as she rifled through and folded the last of the jackets. So far, she had found nothing to worry or upset her but, in feeling in the top pocket of the jacket, a black linen casual, she drew out a business card, the front of which was dominated by the image of a black cat. On the reverse was the strap line *The Nightclub for Sophisticats* together with address and phone number.

She did not know what she would learn, if anything, by paying a visit, but she felt compelled to go, driven by the sense that no stone should be left unturned or no avenue unexplored; driven by the desire to find an answer, even if in all probability none would be found.

When Paul Levinson opened the door to her about five o'clock late that afternoon, he recognised her immediately.

"Come through to the office," he said. "I was half-expecting you."

Alice followed, brow furrowed in incomprehension, nerves on edge, instincts heightened.

"Sit down," Levinson said.

"I'm..." began Alice.

"I know who you are and I've a shrewd idea why you're here. You're Brett's ex and you and your new boyfriend are wondering where he is. Where is the wayward priest, by the way? Learned his lesson? Too scared to come? Abandoned you?"

Alice was alarmed. "But how do you...?"

"Know?" replied Levinson. "It's my duty to know

when people start interfering in things they should keep well out of. And it's my job to ensure something is done about it."

He picked up a paper knife and flexed it.

"Where is Brett?" said Alice, trying to hold her nerve, half-believing for a moment that he might still be alive.

"You don't need to know where he is. What you really want to know is what state he is in." Alice looked at Levinson, her eyes widening. "He's dead. And you did it."

Alice brought her hands to her mouth to stifle a cry. She tried to hold back the tears but they began to flow, as though the sluice had opened to take the pressure off the dam wall.

"Oh, joyous are the tears of relief," intoned Levinson in a pseudo-religious manner. "But please don't enjoy the feeling too long," his tone darkening.

Alice wiped her eyes. "I don't understand any of it, why he wasn't there, how you know who I am, what he's involved in, Bristol. Nothing. Nothing. I understand nothing." Her words were spitting out like machine gun bullets.

"Ignorance is bliss," said Levinson. "All you need to understand is that you are responsible for killing a man. The current tariff for that would be somewhere between two and ten years, depending on your lawyer and how you flash your eyes or legs at the judge."

Alice looked appalled, trying to take in the enormity of

the predicament.

"You really ought to look on me as your saviour," continued Levinson. "Saving your skin, saving your job, saving your future. By removing Brett's body I have saved, if it's not too melodramatic to say, your life."

"The police are looking for him," said Alice.

"They are doing their job. They will seek but they will not find," replied Levinson.

"They came round looking for his phone," said Alice.

"As I said, they will seek."

"So it was you that broke in," said Alice.

Levinson shrugged. "Needs must. But hey ho, it is clear that you did not tell them the truth. You would not be here otherwise. You would be in some interview room or cell awaiting the wheels of justice to trundle inexorably on."

"But what if I tell them that you…"

"What? Removed a body and a phone. How ridiculous would you look. You have killed a person. You have lied by omission. There is nothing, absolutely nothing to tie me to Barron. You would be thought mad. You might instead be looking at an indeterminate term in a lunatic asylum.

Then, again, someone might think there's a conspiracy involving your priest friend. That you killed Barron, disposed of his body so that you can continue your illicit affair. Very plausible. Very good headlines." Levinson smiled at the scenario.

Alice sat there feeling trapped and defeated.

"But don't worry," said Levinson, tapping the knife on the desk, then picking up an envelope and slicing it slowly open, "nothing will happen."

Alice looked at him.

"Because you will not say anything. You can't afford to. And it is in my interests to say nothing. You will leave here. You will never see me or attempt to contact me again. You will live with the consequences of your actions, but I wouldn't let that weigh too heavily on you. One way or the other, Barron was on the fast track to oblivion. Now, if you don't mind, I have plenty to do. I'll show you out the back door. Seems more appropriate somehow."

Levinson stood. Alice followed.

As the door shut behind her, she found herself in an alley. It took her a while to orientate herself but, once she had cleared her head, it was obvious which direction she had to take.

63

Lee Thompson was on the forecourt checking the signage on the stock and making notes when Levinson pulled up.

"Don't look so alarmed, Lee. Mr. Stevens has asked me to lend you the benefit of my expertise, so I'm here as your guide and mentor. Isn't that convenient?" Levinson pointed to the building. "We need to talk. I won't keep you long."

Inside the office, Levinson was flicking through a folder. "The sales look good, Lee but Sharon on reception is looking miserable. Might be hard, Lee, but try to make her feel good. She's the first thing customers see and in this business you don't get a second chance to make a first impression."

"Yes, Mr. Levinson."

"There's another auction, tomorrow. You know the format. Everything to go ahead as usual. However, this time Mr. Stevens will be showing an interest." Lee's eyes narrowed and lips twisted in consternation. "You may even bump into him, but don't worry if you do. Be polite, courteous, surprised but untroubled. Just do everything as you did before. Pick up the new car and make the deliveries. Understood?"

Lee nodded.

"You're doing well, Lee. Mr. Stevens will be pleased."

On the way out, Levinson leaned over the reception desk and said, "Sharon, you look wonderful today."

Sharon pouted her lips and primped her hair, smiled and blushed. "Thank you, Mr Levinson."

He turned and left. She looked to Lee. Her face dropped; her eyes dulled.

***

"Your instincts were right, Mr. Stevens. There does seem to be something not quite right at Town and Country Motors," said Levinson.

"I knew it, Paul. Go on," said Stevens.

"I think young Thompson is a chip off the old block and is following where Barron led."

"I knew it," said Stevens again, switching the phone to his left ear and picking up a pen.

"I'm not sure what it is, but I suspect it's drugs and the centre of the trade is Bristol Car Auctions."

"It must be that that got Ritchie killed. That's what he was going to tell me," said Stevens, convinced of his certainty.

"I don't know, but it's possible, Mr. Stevens." Levinson was toying with the knight on the board in front of him. "The thing is, Mr. Stevens, there is an auction tomorrow. Lee will be attending it. If you were there you might get an idea what's going on. Lee won't be expecting you, so you might be able to get something from his reaction, how he conducts himself, who he meets, whatever."

"You're right, Paul. Email me the directions and details and I'll be there."

"Will you be taking the Jag?" asked Levinson, lightly.

"Yes, but I won't be selling it," quipped Stevens, and then more earnestly, "Good man, Paul. If what you say is true that would account not only for Ritchie's death, but Barron's disappearance. It looks like that man had something to hide."

"It looks like he wasn't to be trusted, Mr. Stevens," said Levinson.

He put the phone down and moved the knight into a position from which there would be no escape for the king. Then he picked up his phone again. He had a couple more calls to make.

64

Late the next afternoon there was an air of concentrated study in the office. Turner was at her computer, checking video footage; Sheldon was studying and collating the notes made by him and Benson; Benson and Kate were looking at the collation board.

"The more you look at it," said Kate, "the more this is a spider's web of interconnected threads."

"Agreed, ma'am."

"The threads aren't yet strong enough to lead to the spider, but whichever way you cut it, at the heart of this web is this man." Kate tapped her finger on the photo of Levinson. "He is the only one that connects the present and the past. He is the one that knows both murder victims and Brett Barron. He has alibis for the murders and there's no direct link to Barron's disappearance. But he has got to be the key to this."

Benson was not convinced. "But ma'am, this sounds like a big operation and behind every big operation is a Daddy Big Bucks and the only person fitting that bill is Mr. Big House Big Wig himself: George Stevens."

"I'm sorry. I can't see that, Sergeant. Not unless he's a great actor or a double agent," said Kate.

"Like a small wager, ma'am."

"No thank you, Sergeant. I wouldn't want to impoverish you in your retirement."

Suddenly, two events occurred in close proximity to break the air of studious contemplation.

"Ma'am! Papa!" shouted Constable Turner, rising from her chair. "I think I've got something!"

All heads turned to her.

"Papa?" queried Kate.

"Sorry, ma'am. Private joke," said Turner, blushing. "But look. Look at this. I've got two images. One from a bit of private phone footage; one from a CCTV camera on Canal Street about a quarter of a mile from The Black Cat."

The team gathered round Turner's computer. The air was tense with excitement.

"First the private footage," said Turner. "This is taken outside the club in the queue. If you look over the shoulder of the girl in the foreground you can just make out a figure in a hoodie approaching Ritchie. There's a quick movement. A shuffle maybe. Then that's it. It's a little clearer in close-up." Turner rolled the mouse.

"Okay, good," said Kate. "But we can't see a face. At least it's something though."

"Now look at this," said Turner. She pulled up the black and white images from a street camera. A hooded figure was walking briskly towards the camera. The head was bowed but, just at the moment of passing, the figure reached inside the jacket, drew out an object and almost simultaneously pulled back the head covering. A moment later the figure was beyond the camera.

"Wow!" exhaled Sheldon.

Without being told, Turner expanded the image. The bigger the picture, the grainier it became, but Turner froze it at the moment the hood was pulled back.

"I've seen him before somewhere," mused Kate.

"And we've just met him," said Benson, leaving the moment to Turner.

"That is Lee Thompson, new manager of Town and Country Motors," said Turner with a smile on her face.

"And son of the mayor," said Kate.

"And that looks like a knife he's pulled out," said Sheldon.

"Which is probably now in the canal," said Benson.

"Fantastic work. Well done, Fiona," said Kate.

But before anything further was said, the office door burst open and in flew Superintendent Fordyce. He had the look of a demented goose. He was flapping his arms, but he wasn't honking. Struggling for breath, his voice was part way between a donkey with a digestive problem and a cornered rat.

"I've just been speaking to Bristol Police. They've

arrested George Stevens for being in possession of two kilos of high grade cocaine. They said he's claiming to be a personal friend of mine. For God's sake Inspector Brown, sort it out."

"Joe, you come with me," said Kate. "Ian and Fiona, go and pull in Thompson."

"Yes, ma'am," said Benson, turning to Turner and starting to sing the refrain *We're in the Money* before jauntily setting off.

Kate shook her head. "We'll see." She picked up her belongings and followed.

***

Kate looked through the observation window. George Stevens was sitting next to the duty solicitor. His jacket was resting on the back of his chair. His shirt looked as crumpled as his face.

Stevens looked up as Kate and Sheldon entered. A momentary relief came to his face. "Kate," he began.

"Inspector Brown," replied Kate.

"Where's Norman? I was expecting Norman," said Stevens.

"Superintendent Fordyce is otherwise engaged," returned Kate.

Stevens' face slumped. "This is a huge mistake. I'm innocent. I want to get out of here," he said, but the energy was draining from his voice.

"Mr. Stevens, I know the seriousness of the charges against you. I'm here at the invitation of the Bristol Police because of links with other investigations we are conducting."

"What links?" said Stevens, seeking comprehension.

"We'll come to that. But first, Mr. Stevens can you tell me how you came to be in possession of two kilos of high grade cocaine?"

Stevens exhaled, as though exhausted, having to tell once more something he'd told many times before.

"As I told your colleagues, I was looking into whether my businesses were being used for illegal activities. I came to believe that the manager of Town and Country Motors may have been involved in drugs. I attended the car auction to see what went on. On the surface everything seemed alright but as I was leaving the site, I was stopped by the police. The car was searched, drugs were found, and here I am."

"Just to confirm, Mr. Stevens," said Kate, " the manager of Town and Country is?"

"Lee Thompson. Only been with me a short time."

"What put you on to him?" said Kate.

"First of all, I was hoping to find something concrete from what Ritchie Goodwin was going to tell me. Then my suspicions were confirmed by another of my employees, Paul Levinson."

"So, it was Levinson who suggested you go to the auctions," said Kate.

"Yes," said Stevens.

"You claim you are innocent, Mr. Stevens."

"I am," protested Stevens.

"Then has it occurred to you that you were set up. The reason you were stopped was from information received from an anonymous phone call. Who would do that? Who would know where you were?"

"Levinson?" Stevens questioned. He shook his head in disbelief. "No! No! No! It can't be. He's the only one who is straight. The only one I can trust."

"You might have to think again, Mr. Stevens," said Kate.

Stevens looked from Kate to Sheldon and back again. He was searching for truth and understanding but his eyes began to sting as though pricked with sand in a desert storm. He tried to wipe his eyes but he couldn't stop the tears coming or his body heaving with the weight of despair.

When he had settled, Kate continued, "You will be interested to know that Lee Thompson is currently being arrested for the murder of Ritchie Goodwin."

Stevens looked up surprised, then hopeful.

"Well there you are. He's the bad one. He must be the one Ritchie was going to tell me about. Get the truth out of him. Let me go!"

"Not that simple, I'm afraid, Mr. Stevens. You are in a serious predicament. You are under arrest and you have been charged. In fact, your arrest ties up a lot of loose ends."

"How? What loose ends?" said Stevens, crestfallen.

"I suggest you get a very good lawyer, Mr. Stevens, because when this case comes to court, and it will come to that, the prosecution will paint you in the darkest hue."

Stevens stood up. "Where's Norman? I demand to see Norman."

"I am afraid there will be no recourse to old friendships, Mr. Stevens."

"Well, arrest Levinson then," said Stevens frantically.

"We have no reason to. The prosecution would say you are bandying names about to save yourself. They will argue that you are the Mr. Big in drug delivery and supply in the south west. They will say that you used your car business as a front for delivery. They will say that you arranged for the murder of Ritchie Goodwin because he was getting too near the truth; that you rewarded Lee Thompson by giving him the managership of the car business to ensure continuity. They will say you caused the disappearance of Brett Barron and suggest, perhaps, it was Brett Barron who made the anonymous call to get his own back for wrongs received. Finally, they might tie you to the death of Geordie Graham, whose assassination you ordered because he had crossed you."

"Geordie Graham? Who's that? Never heard of him," said Stevens.

"That may be, Mr. Stevens," said Kate, " but when the picture is painted in a jury's mind, what do you think they will think?"

Stevens slumped. He turned to the duty solicitor and said, "I want the best lawyer, now. Whatever it costs, I want the very best, now!"

***

On the solemn trip back up the motorway, Sheldon said, "He's innocent, you know"

"I know," said Kate.

"It's Levinson, isn't it?" said Sheldon.

"We can't prove it," replied Kate.

Sheldon shook his head. "There's no justice. You could say he's got away with murder." He pressed his foot hard on the accelerator.

"Yes," said Kate, to herself as much as to Sheldon. She remained silent, lost in thought for the remainder of the journey.

***

Benson and Turner were at Laurel Close with

reinforcements. Two uniformed officers were deployed to the back of the house to prevent escape through the school field. Two were at the front door with a steel ram. All were dressed in body armour.

On Benson's signal, the door was rammed. There was a mighty crack of wood and shattering of glass.

Inside the house there was silence. Benson led the way to the kitchen where the four officers came upon a family scene.

Seated at the table were Mr. and Mrs. Johnny Thompson. Mr. Thompson sat in his underclothes. He was unshaven. He was looking blankly at the chains of office on the table before him. He turned to look at the officers. His eyes had the distant look of a cod on a fishmonger's stall. Opposite him sat Mrs. Thompson, puffy faced and unkempt hair, cradling and soothing as a mother might a baby, the decaying carcase of a cat. Standing up by the kitchen sink was Lee Thompson. He looked relaxed. He was sipping tea. He was in no hurry.

The air was pungent with decay.

Benson turned to Turner and indicated with his hand that she had a job to do.

Turner approached Lee. "Lee Thompson. You are under arrest for the murder of Ritchie Goodwin. You do not have to say anything. But, it may harm your defence if you do not mention when questioned something which you later rely on in court. Anything you do say may be given in evidence."

She produced a pair of handcuffs from a pouch on her belt.

Thompson put out his arms, stiff from the shoulders, like a cartoon sleepwalker. He smiled. "Yeah. Whatever. Bring it on."

As Thompson was being led away, Mrs. Thompson brought her hand to her mouth and giggled uncontrollably.

65

Superintendent Fordyce scurried past the collation board where Kate was taking down the pictures and erasing the notes. He did not want to be disturbed. He was on a mission to distance himself from any connection with the personages involved in these cases.

As Kate was detaching the photo of Paul Levinson, her phone buzzed to indicate a text had arrived. It was a withheld number. The message consisted of a few words and a telephone number. The words said: *For justice, contact*.

For a moment Kate was nonplussed but as she glanced from her phone to the board, she saw the picture of the army pals, celebrating. She knew then what she had to do.

On her way home that evening she posted an envelope to Florence Chambers at Highfield. Inside there was nothing but a photograph of Levinson and a transcription of the text message.

66

Alice was sombre. She was sitting at a table in Mama's Italian Café. She was holding her hands and looking down at them. She had just related to Wyatt everything that Levinson had told her.

"So, I did kill him," she said. "What's going to happen now?"

She looked up and their eyes locked. Wyatt stretched his hands across the table and took both of hers in his.

"I'm not a priest," he said, "so I can't offer absolution. But I can offer myself and a future."

Their eyes welled and gentle smiles played on their faces.

"Where?" Alice said.

"First, Carlisle, then the world," replied Wyatt.

67

The board was set. Pawn to king four. The best games always begin with the simplest of moves, he thought, and smiled.

68

That evening, Kate was on the sofa with Misha cuddled up beside her. They had enjoyed the children's tv programme just before the early evening news.

"Mummy, can I make tea?" said Misha.

"That would be lovely," said Kate. "What do you have in mind?"

"Pancakes," enthused Misha.

"You make the mix and I'll come and help in a few minutes."

Misha bounded from the sofa.

Kate looked away from the television to the smiling face of Captain Martin Brown and wondered when the call would come through.

Thanks

To Jenny who said I had no excuse; to my early readers in the family and friends who offered encouragement and suggested clarifications; to Alasdair and Don of the Blokes' Book Club, sharp readers both; and to Terry without whose skill and technical wizardry you would not be reading this at all.

Patrick T. Groome

About the author

The author lives in Oxfordshire

Printed in Great Britain
by Amazon